Bolan dropp[ed] single bullet [to] [the] [chest]

If it was blood they wanted, the Executioner was ready to provide it. He would teach his enemies a lesson about taking victory for granted. Even if they killed him, survivors of the skirmish would remember, and perhaps take something with them from the carnage when they fled.

He hadn't meant for this to happen, but the choice was made. His foes had called the play, but they would not control the game.

Bolan lined up his weapon on the trail and listened to the hunters, careless in their haste. That racket was another costly error. The only question, now, was whether any of the trackers would survive to learn from their mistakes.

Or whether Bolan would survive to see another day.

MACK BOLAN ®
The Executioner

The Executioner®
Don Pendleton's
JUNGLE JUSTICE

A GOLD EAGLE BOOK FROM
WORLDWIDE®

TORONTO • NEW YORK • LONDON
AMSTERDAM • PARIS • SYDNEY • HAMBURG
STOCKHOLM • ATHENS • TOKYO • MILAN
MADRID • WARSAW • BUDAPEST • AUCKLAND

First edition September 2006
ISBN-13: 978-0-373-64334-9
ISBN-10:   0-373-64334-9

Special thanks and acknowledgment to
Michael Newton for his contribution to this work.

JUNGLE JUSTICE

There is no forgiveness in nature.
—Ugo Betti, 1892–1953
Crime on Goat Island

Nature takes care of her own, but we sometimes can't afford to wait. This time, I'm helping to level the scales.
—Mack Bolan

For the Linkup, fighting for justice one step at a time.

Prologue

Sundarbans Wildlife Park, India

"I'm still not clear exactly why we need an army escort in a game preserve," Phillip Langley said.

His guide, a thirty-something diplomat named Rajit Singh, concealed any frustration that he may have felt concerning Langley's poor retention. Smiling, he replied, "All wildlife is protected in the Sundarbans, and most particularly tigers, sir. Of course, the law is one thing, and reality is something else entirely, as I'm sure you know."

Joyce Langley spoke up from the seat beside her husband, swaying with the rocking motion of their boat as it moved ever deeper into the world's largest mangrove swamp. "You mean that poachers hunt the tigers, even here?" she asked.

"Most certainly, memsahib," the guide replied. "And here most cunningly of all."

Stomach uneasy, Phillip Langley asked, "When do we go ashore?"

"Not long, sir," Singh assured him. "Fifteen minutes, maybe less."

The heat was even more oppressive here than in Calcutta, where Langley and his wife had spent the previous night in what passed for a four-star hotel, after meeting their guide at the local seat of government. Langley's role as special U.S.

envoy and a member of the President's task force on preservation of endangered species had assured Langley the best room in the house—which wasn't saying much.

At least, he reassured himself, it was a far cry from the teeming, reeking slums they'd seen while driving from the airport to their rendezvous with Rajit Singh. Langley was clueless as to how people survived in squalor so profound and hopeless. Given half a chance, he would've filmed Calcutta in 3-D, bottled its smell and shared the grim experience with everyone who ranted about poverty in the United States.

Compared to the worst of Calcutta, the South Bronx and Cabrini Green looked like a juicy slice of *Beverly Hills, 90210*. Langley wasn't sure that any of the people he'd seen lying in the streets and gutters had been *dead*, but on the other hand, living in such conditions made the prospect of a coronary sound like sweet relief.

Now, here they were, sweating beneath a broiling sun, the humidity close to one hundred percent, and his industrial-strength bug repellent was barely holding the king-sized mosquitoes at bay. They'd seen some birds that Langley didn't recognize, and several crocodiles that eyed him as if he was a prospective snack.

Even with the rocking of the boat, Langley had almost soured on the plan to go ashore. Ideally, he'd have ordered Singh to turn the boat around and take them back to the Port Canning railhead, but how would that look in his final report?

Stiff upper lip, he thought, wiping the perspiration from it with his sleeve.

"I understand most of the tigers in the Sundarbans are man-eaters," his wife was saying, using all of her considerable charm on Rajit Singh.

"You are correct, memsahib," the guide replied. "That is another reason for the military guard, you know. Because prey in the game preserve is scarce, and humans run so slowly, most of the three hundred Bengal tigers here have eaten men. We record an average twenty-six maulings per year, most of them fishermen and woodcutters."

"And still, you work to save the tigers?"

"But of course. It is the law." Raising an arm to point, Singh told them, "There, ahead, you see the dock where we will land."

Langley could see the dock, all right, but he felt less secure than ever about stepping from the boat. Twenty-six tiger kills in a year meant one every two weeks. When had the last one been, he wondered. Was it time to log a fresh statistic on the butcher's bill?

The boat was veering toward the dock on his left. Langley knew he was running out of time. "About these tigers, Mr. Singh," he said. "What happens if we meet one on our tour? I mean, if we meet a *hungry* one."

Singh smiled at that, just short of mocking him. "Fear not, sir. We have the pistols without bullets—oh, what do you call them?"

"Starter pistols?"

"Yes! We have the starter pistols and electric prods. Is very safe."

"But we have rifles, too," Langley reminded him, eyeing their uniformed escort.

"Rifles are only for the poachers and the bandits, sir." Singh's tone was solemn now. "We shoot a tiger only as the very last resort, sir, in a most extreme emergency. And even then, I fear my job is forfeit."

"Still," Langley insisted, "in a real emergency—"

"Have no fear, sir." The guide had found his smile. "I have not lost a Western diplomat so far."

"So far?"

"Joking! We have the laugh together, yes?"

Hilarious, Langley thought, as he forced a smile. Joyce

poked him in the ribs, a subtle elbow shot, and he managed to say, "That's quite a wit you've got there, Mr. Singh."

The guide beamed at him. "Everyone is telling me the same, sir. If I was not in the government employ, I should be a comedian."

"Something to think about," Langley replied. *In case a tiger eats my ass.*

The boat nosed in against the dock, where some native youths stood waiting to secure the lines. More soldiers also stood by, rifles slung or tucked beneath their arms, guarding a pair of Land Rovers.

"There are no highways in the Sundarbans," Singh told them, when they stood once more on semisolid ground, "and few passable roads. To really see the game preserve, a person must walk or travel on the waterways, but I believe you would prefer to ride."

You got that right, Langley thought. *If I have to be among man-eating tigers, lock me in a sturdy SUV.*

"That's very thoughtful of you," Joyce said.

"Sadly, the Rovers have no air-conditioning," Singh said, "but we shall roll the windows down. Only a few tigers jump through the windows of a moving vehicle." He let them soak that in, then said, "I joke again!"

"Better and better," Langley said. "About those gangs you mentioned—"

"Mostly poachers," Singh replied. "Mostly a group led by the pig Naraka. My apologies, memsahib."

"Naraka?" Langley asked.

"A bad man. Very bad. But have no fear, sir. I believe we shall not meet with him today."

1

Calcutta

Calcutta was a shock to any first-time Western visitor.

It was the second-most populous city in an overcrowded nation where more than thirteen million people shared barely eight hundred square miles.

Over the past two centuries, the city had been purged by floods, famine, riots and war. The British influence remained—English predominated on street signs and in public conversation—but the constitution also recognized fifteen other tongues. Great religions rubbed shoulders in the crowded streets, but the ancient image of death goddess Kali was never far removed, her six arms reaching out for skulls and human sacrifice.

Above all, there was poverty. Calcutta's slums dwarfed those of Bangkok, Jakarta, Rangoon or Kuala Lumpur. Millions roamed and slept on filthy streets, dressed in rags and infected with loathsome diseases, living hand-to-mouth as thieves or beggars. Others sold themselves, either for sex or literally, piece by piece, to blood and organ vendors representing wealthy clients. What did a cornea or kidney matter, when the final stakes were life or death?

Mack Bolan had passed through Asian slums before, in half a dozen troubled nations, but Calcutta's were the worst he had

seen. The odors permeated flesh and fabric, defying the purga-
tive powers of soap and shampoo. There was a kind of soul-
rot in this place that crept inside the human heart and
burrowed deep.

Bolan had flown in early from the States to learn the
ground before he met his contact and began the mission
proper. Lack of preparation was a fatal flaw in the Executioner's trade, where each decision had a direct impact on his
longevity. He'd managed to survive this far, against long odds,
by paying close attention to details.

And he didn't intend to change that pattern now.

Calcutta had its stylish neighborhoods, department stores
and monuments, but none of that concerned him. Bolan's
path lay on the wild side, in the darkness where "respectable"
Calcuttans seldom strayed, a part of their immediate sur-
roundings they struggled daily to ignore.

Bolan's hotel was an outpost on the DMZ between tourist-
brochure Calcutta and a blighted district where the "other
half" sometimes didn't survive the night. His first foray across
the line, made on the afternoon of his arrival, was a visit to a
certain shop on the wrong end of Benjamin Disraeli Street.
Ostensibly, the owner was a pawnbroker who earned his living from the misfortune of others, but his secret back room
was an arsenal of modern military hardware, open to selected
customers by invitation only.

Bolan's invitation was a roundabout arrangement, courtesy
of Hal Brognola at Justice and a colleague with the CIA in
Langley, Virginia. A word to the wise, and Bolan was in, shar-
ing the wealth he'd lifted from a Baltimore crack dealer two
weeks earlier to purchase certain basics of the soldier's trade.

His purchases included a Steyr AUG assault rifle, chambered for the same 5.56 mm rounds used in the native INSAS
models, but more compact and reliable in adverse conditions.
For his side arm, he'd chosen a Glock 17, again taking a

weapon chambered for the common 9 mm round used by Indian police and military personnel, but with a reputation for superior performance under rough handling. Spare magazines for both weapons, a shoulder harness for the Glock, plus ammunition and a brand-new K-Bar fighting knife had rounded off his purchase.

He had stashed the AUG and various accessories at his hotel, but wore the Glock when he went out to learn the city's secrets. Bolan knew, before he set foot on the sidewalk, that a lifetime could be spent trying to understand Calcutta, yet the deepest, darkest secrets would evade him. That was fine, as long as he picked up enough to help him stay alive to complete his mission.

Police patrols, for instance. Bolan marked them, noted where the prowl cars went and where they didn't, which blocks were ignored and left to fester with no uniforms in sight. He was convinced that several of the sleeping men he passed along his way were dead, in fact, but Bolan didn't stop to prove the point.

None of his business. He had other work to do.

His contact had arranged a meeting at a curry restaurant, a quarter mile from Bolan's small hotel. He had studied three approaches to the place, which occupied a busy corner in a kind of low-rent no-man's land. He could approach his target from the north or south, along Clarke Street, or from the east, by passing through a squalid alleyway perversely labeled London Mews. He recognized the alley as a prime spot for an ambush, but the crowded north-south street was just as bad, if someone cared enough to infiltrate the crowd of passersby or fire from the apartments stacked above street-level shops.

The one thing Bolan absolutely didn't plan to do that night was to dine on curry in an unfamiliar restaurant. He had a cast-iron stomach, long inured to gagalicious Green Beret cuisine, but still he didn't want to take the chance. Instead, he ate a midday meal at his hotel and made it last, bolstered by shrink-wrapped snacks and bottled water in the early evening, as daylight waned.

Bolan put on his stern game face and hit the streets with an hour to spare, ample time to reach his destination, scout the neighborhood one last time and be ready when his contact finally arrived. The image of a passport photograph was burned into his memory, a common face, but one he would not forget until the mission was behind him and he had no further need of it.

The sat phone in his pocket was a hot line to the States, with Hal Brognola's several numbers and Stony Man Farm on speed dial, but none of them would help him here. Bolan was off the screen this evening, well and truly on his own.

ABHAYA TAKERI WAS EARLY for his rendezvous with the American. Unlike the stranger he had come to meet, he had no photographs to work from, not even a physical description of the man who'd traveled halfway around the world to meet him in Calcutta. But he had the magic word.

Saffron.

Someone had thought about it and decided it would be the perfect password for a meeting in a restaurant. Why not? They didn't pay Takeri to decide such things, only to speak the words that he was given and perform on cue in other ways.

This night, and for the next few days, he would be serving the American as travel guide, interpreter, and general font of knowledge on the ins and outs of life in West Bengal. Beyond that—if he had to fight, for instance—they would have to renegotiate.

Takeri hoped that it would be a simple job, but he already had his doubts. His briefing had included details that suggested travel far afield. He didn't mind leaving the city—he was a former country boy himself—but there were dangers in the hinterland that made Calcutta's numbing misery pale by comparison.

He knew tourists imagined India as quaint and scenic, with men in turbans and pith helmets riding elephants around plantations, in the shadow of the Taj Mahal. Landmarks aside, their vision of Takeri's homeland came primarily from 1940s Hollywood, doubly distorted through a camera's lens and a kaleidoscope of wishful thinking, harking back to times that never were. The West had lost control of India in 1947, and that stranglehold was never the idyllic life portrayed in films or novels. The common Western view of India was no more accurate than the portrait of American slavery painted in *Gone With the Wind*.

Before his grandfather's great-grandfather was born, Takeri's homeland was invaded, subjugated and exploited for the benefit of merchants and their lackeys, living half a world away. The native culture was suppressed, where it conflicted with the flow of tribute back to London, brutality and wholesale slaughter brought to bear when "insurrectionists" fought back. The history of India was written in her people's blood, spilled by conquerors who left their imprint on the land, the language, everything he saw and touched from day to day.

Takeri's nationalism didn't mark him as a die-hard enemy of the West, however. He recognized that there were troubles enough in his homeland, without blaming anyone outside India's borders. Gandhi himself had never managed to quell the sectarian bloodshed between Hindus, Sikhs and Muslims that continued to the present day. That three-way war had claimed Indira Gandhi's life and countless others, since the British tyrants had withdrawn in 1947. It endured still, in clashes over Kashmir, with the Pakistanis, and echoed in the living tragedy of Bangladesh. Too many children still labored in virtual slavery, while untouchables were scorned and persecuted, women slain in honor killings by their jealous husbands or else immolated when their spouses died.

Change for the better was a slow and agonizing process. Abhaya Takeri shared the frustration of his countrymen who wanted better lives without surrendering the best parts of their native culture. He believed such things were possible. And that, in part, was what had opened him to contract offers from the CIA.

He recognized the irony of his complaints against the West, while he collected U.S. dollars for his service to the lords of Washington. Sometimes he woke up in the middle of the night, from troubled dreams, seething with anger at himself and at the nation that had forced him toward a measure of betrayal. In the end, though, when it mattered most, Takeri managed to persuade himself that he was working for a greater good, on behalf of India and all her people.

This time, for example, if his briefing had been accurate, he would assist in cleaning out a nest of bandit scum who had disgraced West Bengal for over a decade. Poaching was only part of it, an outlawed trade that spawned corruption, theft and murder stretching from Calcutta to the Sundarbans.

How many lives had Balahadra Naraka claimed so far? Two hundred? Three hundred or more? Takeri wasn't sure, and further doubted that precise statistics were important. Various officials in West Bengal had been negligent or worse in dealing with the problem, throwing up their hands and pleading helplessness in the face of Naraka's savagery. Their failure was a national disgrace, one Abhaya Takeri hoped to remedy.

While waiting for his meet with the American, he'd made inquiries here and there, around Calcutta. Certain merchants knew when contraband was moving, knew the sellers and buyers, their middlemen, the details necessary to unravel a conspiracy. With coaxing, he had managed to unlock their lips, extract their secrets bit by bit. More remained to be exposed, but for the moment, he was satisfied.

If only he could shake the sense of being followed.

There was nothing he could point to with assurance, no familiar face glimpsed time and time again behind him, in a crowd. But still, Takeri *knew* someone was watching him. He had a special sense about such matters, which had saved his life on more than one occasion. As he approached the curry restaurant, Takeri was alert to any shadows, spotting none.

He could abort the meeting, leave some message with the restaurant's proprietor for the American to try another place, another time, but that would start them on the wrong foot, make the stranger feel Takeri was incompetent. Perhaps, he told himself, the feeling was just that—a feeling without substance. If he couldn't see his enemies, Takeri knew there was at least a chance that they did not exist.

He dawdled through the last four blocks, still early for the meeting, killing time at shop windows and shrugging off the beggars who infested Clarke Street. None was quite so forward as to touch Takeri, but they crowded him, pleading for money or anything else he could spare. Takeri ignored them, brushing past them as if they didn't exist, and felt the worse for it with every step he took.

He felt the beggars studied him and mocked him while he window-shopped and several times reversed directions, hoping by that method to detect a stranger following. Takeri wondered if the poor and starving thought him mad, then finally decided that it made no difference. Their opinion didn't matter. It was nothing, written on the wind.

A short block from the restaurant, he was almost persuaded that his fears were all in vain. He'd been mistaken. There was no one after him at all. Why should there be?

And then, two men emerged from London Mews, moving to block his path. They were not beggars, and the hands they offered to him were not held palm-up and empty.

Both were clutching knives.

Takeri stopped, began to turn and glimpsed two other men he had somehow missed, closing behind him now. Long blades sprouted from their dark fists.

Cursing himself for carelessness, Takeri realized he was about to die.

2

The Executioner had started to relax at the first glimpse of his contact. The man was taking his time and double-checking to be sure he wasn't followed. That was something Bolan could appreciate, a conscientious guide to help him through the next few days.

He wouldn't jump the gun, Bolan decided, wouldn't try to brace his contact on the sidewalk, when they'd already agreed to meet inside the restaurant. It was a small thing, but he didn't want to start off breaking rules, changing established orders. It created a bad precedent, and Bolan didn't want to go there.

He was patient, giving his connection time to reach the restaurant and go inside, when Bolan saw two men emerge from London Mews, the stinking alley paved with trash. Both moved to intercept his contact, and the young man saw them, blinking once before he thought about retreat—and found himself cut off behind by two more men.

It wasn't Bolan's fault, but self-recrimination still flashed through his mind. He hadn't seen the followers, because they got lost in the teeming sidewalk crowd, but he could easily have checked the alley one more time, or even waited there himself to watch his contact pass.

Now the young man was ringed by hostile faces, and the four men who'd surrounded him were armed with knives.

Damn it!

Their first maneuver barely caused an eddy in the flow of foot traffic, then someone saw the blades and started shouting in a high-pitched voice. Bolan didn't speak the shouter's language, but he got the drift.

He knew only one way to trump four blades, and that was with a gun. It wasn't how he'd meant to hook up with his contact, but the circumstances had been forced upon him by third parties. Bolan could do nothing but react, as swiftly and effectively as possible.

He palmed the Glock, holding it against his thigh as he proceeded, none too gently, through the sidewalk crowd. After retreating to a distance safe from random slashes, most of the immediate bystanders had decided they should watch the unexpected scene play out, rather than running for a cop or for their lives. The police might have been summoned, even so—Calcutta had its share of cell phones, just like any other city on the planet—and whatever Bolan meant to do, he knew he'd have to do it soon.

His first concern was no careless shooting in the crowd. His weapon didn't have the penetration power of a Magnum, but a hot 9 mm load might still go through one man and strike another, if he wasn't careful. Even warning shots were dangerous—they had to come down somewhere—and the very sound of gunfire might provoke a stampede that would force him away from his contact, instead of allowing him access.

Rather than firepower, therefore, Bolan first relied on muscle power, charging through the crowd and bulling human obstacles aside. Some snapped at him, presumably cursing, but he paid no heed. His contact was about to be filleted, and Bolan meant to stop it if he could.

If he wasn't too late.

The four blade men were circling when he reached them by bursting through the final row of onlookers. One of the goons, directly opposite, saw Bolan coming in a rush and tried to warn his comrades, but the nearest didn't get the word in time. The slicer's first inkling of trouble was the tight grip of a strong hand on his shoulder, spinning him, before the Glock's butt smashed into his face.

Some of the gawkers saw the pistol and withdrew from the epicenter of the action, but they still made no attempt to flee en masse. They seemed addicted to the show and would stay to see its end unless he started firing, forcing them to run for cover.

The attackers, still in fighting form, were torn between two targets and mindful of the gun in Bolan's hand. They couldn't read him yet, beyond a safe guess that he wasn't a policeman, but they had no time to think about the riddle. Bolan, for his part, already wondered if the street attack had anything to do with him, but there was no way he could find out at that moment.

Fight now, instinct told him, and ask questions later. If you're still alive.

The thug farthest from Bolan lunged at the Executioner's contact with his knife. The young man turned rapidly to meet the thrust and blocked it with one hand, while the other lashed out toward his adversary's face. It was a fair blow, staggering the hoodlum, but it failed to drop him, and a second lightning jab was required to put him on the ground.

That still left two, and one of them apparently decided it was safe to charge Bolan, pitting a six-inch blade against his pistol. The soldier could've double-tapped his enemy with ease, but there were too many civilians ranged behind the target for a guaranteed clean shot. Instead, he braced himself, prepared to meet his would-be killer hand to hand.

The youngster wasn't bad, slashing at Bolan with a move that could've split his face or throat, but in the end he wound up cleaving only air. Bolan had ducked and sidestepped, lashed a kick into his young opponent's groin, and watched the fight bleed out of him as he collapsed onto all fours. It was a simple thing, from there, to whip the Glock across his skull and leave him stretched out on the pavement.

One blade left, and Bolan's contact had it more or less in hand, grappling with his opponent chest-to-chest, arms raised well overhead, the knife's long blade reflecting glints of neon from surrounding signs. With all hands occupied, the two combatants waltzed and waddled, lurching back and forth across the sidewalk, ringed by spectators.

Bolan was moving in to break the standoff, when a gunshot cracked somewhere behind him and the young knife-wielder's head exploded, spattering his adversary with a spray of blood and tissue. Bolan's contact violently recoiled, shoving the corpse away from him, and thereby saved himself from the next shot.

"Get down!" Bolan cried, rushing even as he spoke to grab one of his contact's arms and drag him into London Mews. The young man struggled, fought him, until Bolan shoved him hard against a filthy wall.

"We don't have time for this!" he snapped. "No saffron on the menu, get it? Someone wants you dead. We need to get the hell away from here."

His contact registered the password, blinked at Bolan in surprise, then nodded. "Yes," he said. "I understand. This way!"

The next gunshot was well off target, fired from somewhere on the street into the alley's mouth. It ricocheted off dirty bricks and burrowed into garbage, while the Executioner followed his contact through London Mews. A clutch of beggars tried to intercept them, then fell supine at the sight of Bolan's gun.

They burst from the alley into another crowded street. Calcutta had no other kind, it seemed, and Bolan had mixed feelings for the crush of soiled humanity. Bodies provided cover, but they also clogged his field of fire. Pedestrians might shield him from his unknown enemies—or there might be assassins in the crowd, ready to slip a blade between his ribs.

Without a vehicle or ready options, Bolan trailed his contact south along a street he soon identified as Churchill Boulevard. The street was lined with panhandlers and prostitutes, with a snake charmer performing on the corner just ahead. As they approached the intersection, yet another thug appeared in front of Bolan's guide, this one clutching a stubby pistol in both hands.

Before Bolan could aim and fire, his contact stooped beside the snake charmer, plucked up a startled cobra from the old man's wicker basket, spun and pitched it straight into the shooter's face. Their adversary squealed and dropped his weapon, flailing at the reptile draped around his shoulders.

Bolan left him to it, racing past and following his contact through a hard right turn into another carbon-copy street. They found a recessed doorway, ducked into its shadow, Bolan's contact peering out to check the street behind them.

"That was pretty slick," Bolan said, "with the snake. I didn't catch your name in the excitement."

"Abhaya Takeri," the young man replied. "And yours?"

"Matt Cooper," Bolan said. Today, at least.

"I don't believe we should remain here any longer, Mr. Cooper."

"Where—"

Before Bolan could put his question into words, a bullet struck the wall beside Takeri's head and ricocheted into the street. A woman screamed, perhaps wounded, beyond his line of sight. Takeri turned at once, pushed through the door behind them, Bolan following into a tattoo parlor.

There were two chairs in the shop, both occupied by customers. The tattoo artists looked like twins, emaciated stick figures with matted hair and Fu Manchu mustaches going gray. Between the cloying incense, the whine of tattoo needles and demonic artwork mounted on the walls around him, Bolan felt as if he'd stepped into the third circle of Hell.

One of the artists said something he couldn't understand. Takeri answered curtly and proceeded through the tiny shop toward a back room. They rattled through a screen of dangling beads, hooked left to where the back door stood propped open with a wooden crate and shouldered through into an alley barely wide enough to let them pass in single file.

Bolan had no idea who would construct an alley so narrow, or why, but it appeared to be a dumping trough for litter thrown from windows overhead. Thankfully, most of the discarded refuse had been dry—paper and cardboard, empty cans and bottles, scraps of wood and plaster board—instead of offal and the like. They clambered over knee-high dunes of rubbish, slogging north along the claustrophobic passageway, Takeri hissing steadily for Bolan to keep up.

"I'm right behind you," Bolan said, then ducked as bullets started flying through the alley, gouging furrows in the brick to either side.

He crouched and swiveled, bruised a hip in those close quarters, lining up his Glock on a dark figure at the far end of the alley. Bolan saw the shooter's muzzle-flash and fought the urge to flinch from it, squeezing his pistol's trigger twice in rapid fire.

The echo of his shots was thunderous inside the alley, punctuated by the sound of cartridges rebounding from brick walls. He saw his human target stumble, turn, collapsing on his face. When the shooter did not immediately rise again, Bolan dismissed him, moving on.

Takeri reached the next street, plunged across it without looking left or right, while horse-drawn carts and rickshaws bustled past him. Bolan dodged a battered taxi cab and followed, gaining on Takeri as his contact reached the sidewalk opposite, then ducked into another darkened doorway.

Stairs this time, with people lounging on them, possibly asleep. Takeri hurdled each new obstacle, cursing when one reached out to snag his cuff, kicking to free himself. Another hand found Bolan, tried to grasp his ankle, but it lacked the strength to hold him. Moments later, they were pushing through another door and out onto the building's roof.

"Where to?" Bolan asked, as he paused to catch his breath.

"With luck, they may not find us here," Takeri answered.

Any hope of that was dashed a moment later, with the sound of angry voices and a gunshot from the stairwell. Bolan spun to face the doorway, leveling his pistol, but Takeri stepped in front of him.

"Better to run while we still can," Takeri said.

"Run where?"

"Across the rooftops, there."

Takeri pointed, already in motion as he sprinted toward a nearby parapet and launched himself through space to land on the rooftop of a building to the south. Bolan went after him, immediately thankful for the narrow alleyways that seemed to be Calcutta's fashion. He was tiring, and a broader leap, followed by three or four more of the same, might well have winded him.

They crossed four rooftops, running hard, before Takeri found another open door and led the way down darkened stairs—unoccupied, this time—to reach the street. Bolan had not looked back to see if they were being followed, but he took it as a given. They would have to stand and fight soon, even if Takeri's preference was an all-night run.

Bolan was on the verge of saying so when they emerged onto the crowded sidewalk and his contact hailed a passing cab. The driver stopped at once, and they piled into his back seat, almost as if the ride had been prearranged.

Bolan glanced through the cab's rear window and saw no one in pursuit. Relaxing for the first time in what felt like hours, he sat back and stowed his pistol in its armpit holster.

"So," he asked Takeri, "what was that about?"

"I can't be sure," the younger man replied. "Do you have lodgings in Calcutta?"

Bolan nodded. "Why?"

"Because we need a place to talk, and I no longer trust the streets."

3

Fort McHenry, Baltimore

It had been Bolan's turn to choose the meeting place, and he'd made his selection on a whim. It had to be within an hour's drive of Washington, but within those parameters anything went.

He'd chosen Fort McHenry for its history—"Star Spangled Banner," and all that—as well as its proximity to certain high-crime streets that might prove useful if the call from Hal Brognola concerned another job.

And what else would it be?

Granted, Brognola was a friend of long standing who phoned his regards on holidays, birthdays and such. He couldn't send cards, because Mack Bolan had no fixed address. But a weekday phone call requesting a face-to-face ASAP could only mean work.

And work meant death, no matter how they tried to dress it up in frills.

The fort had been restored with loving care. Tourists could stroll along the parapets where early defenders had cringed from the rocket's red glare, clutching muskets and sabers, most praying they wouldn't be called on to use them.

That had been during the country's second war with Britain, going on two hundred years ago, and Bolan's home-land still hadn't achieved a lasting peace. Its history was scarred by conflict stretching from the shot heard 'round the world to Kabul and Baghdad. The freedoms cherished there were sacrosanct to Bolan, but their price was high.

He wondered, sometimes, what the politicians thought they had achieved, besides securing their own reelection, but it never troubled him for long. The republic had survived good presidents and bad, congressmen who helped the poor and robbed them blind, judges who did their level best and others who were on the take from every scumbag they could find. America endured, sometimes despite its leaders, rather than because of them.

In Bolan's world it was a different story. He'd quit taking orders when he shed his Army uniform and launched a new war of his own, against the syndicated criminals responsible for nearly wiping out his family. That war had taught him things he'd never learned in Special Forces training, and Bolan had taken those lessons to heart.

These days, he was unique among all other warriors he had ever known or studied. The nearest facsimile came from ancient Japan, when masterless samurai called *ronin* traveled at will through a feudal landscape, choosing their battles and renting their swords to the highest bidder.

Bolan wasn't a mercenary, though. He'd cast his lot with Hal Brognola at the Department of Justice, and Brognola's covert-action teams at Stony Man Farm, in the wild Blue Ridge Mountains of Virginia. But he didn't belong to them. Bolan was free to turn down any job that didn't suit him, though he rarely exercised that privilege. In most cases he found that Brognola's concern, his sense of urgency, matched Bolan's own.

That didn't mean he'd want the job the big Fed brought to him this morning, at Fort McHenry. Every time they met, a part of Bolan's mind was ready to decline the mission, picking it apart in search of elements that made it hopeless or unworthy of his time. It was a rare day when he found those elements—not half a dozen times in all the years he'd worked with Hal—but it could happen.

As his compact with Brognola left him free to pick and choose, so it allowed Bolan to chart selected missions of his own, without Brognola's go-ahead. Brognola nearly always backed him to the limit, but they both knew that it wasn't guaranteed, and if the man from Washington said no, it wouldn't be a deal breaker for either of them.

Not yet, anyway.

Moving among the tourists, eavesdropping on fragmentary conversations, Bolan marveled at their ignorance of history. One woman thought Fort McHenry had been shelled by "Communists" during the Civil War. Her male companion solemnly corrected her, insisting the aggressors had been French. Most of the others didn't seem to care what might've happened there, so long ago, as long as they could spend a morning in the sunshine, briefly free from care.

And maybe that, thought Bolan, was the reason many of his nation's battles had been fought.

History books extolled the U.S. combat soldier's dedication to abstractions—Justice, Freedom and Democracy were those most prominently listed. Bolan, for his part, had never met a soldier who spent any barracks time at all debating politics, when there was talk of women, sports or food to be enjoyed. And in the orchestrated panic that was battle, he had never heard a fighting man of either side die with a patriotic slogan on his lips. They asked for wives or lovers, parents, siblings—anyone at all, in fact, except the leaders who had put them on the battlefield.

Armies defended or invaded nations. Soldiers fought to stay alive and help their buddies. Only "statesmen" waged war for ideals, and most of them had never fired a shot in anger, or been fired on in return.

Bolan had once maintained a journal, filled with thoughts about his private wars, the Universe, his place within the scheme of things and mankind's destiny. He'd discontinued it some years ago, more from a lack of idle time than any shift in feeling, and he didn't miss it now.

Who'd ever read or care about his private thoughts, in any case? Officially, he was a dead man, had been since his pyrotechnic finish had been staged by Hal Brognola in New York. From there, he'd been reborn—new face, new life, new war.

Except, in truth, his war had never really changed.

His enemies were predators in human form, who victimized the weak and relatively innocent. Like some unworthy patriots and holy men, they dressed their crimes in disguises of infinite variety. They were left- and right-wing, conservative and liberal, Muslim and Christian, Jew and gentile, male and female, young and old. They came in every color of the human rainbow, but they always wanted the same thing.

Whatever they could steal.

Bolan stood in their way, sometimes alone, sometimes with comrades who were dedicated to the fight for its own sake. And while he knew he couldn't win them all, he'd done all right so far.

He found the spot he'd designated for his meeting with Brognola, leaned against the rough stone of the parapet and settled in to wait. The man from Justice thrived on punctuality, but Bolan was ten minutes early. He had time to kill.

He couldn't see or hear the ghosts who walked those grounds, but Bolan never doubted they were present, bound by pain and sacrifice to the last battleground they'd known in life. And something told him that they didn't really mind.

BROGNOLA STEPPED UP to the wall at Bolan's side, and said "Been waiting long?"

"Not too long," Bolan answered. "Shall we walk?"

"Suits me," Brognola said.

He studied Bolan, as he always did, striving for subtlety. It wasn't good to stare, but he supposed that shooting furtive glances from the corner of his eye would make him seem ridiculous, like something from a Peter Sellers comedy.

"How are you?" he inquired at last.

"Getting along," Bolan replied.

Okay. No small talk, then.

"I've got a project that I thought might suit you, if you're interested," Brognola told him, cutting to the chase.

"Let's hear it."

"What do you know about India?"

Bolan considered it, then said, "Huge population. Sacred cows. Border disputes with Pakistan and China. Trouble with the Sikhs."

"Endangered species?" he suggested, prodding.

Bolan shrugged. "I wouldn't be surprised."

"What about tigers?"

"Big and dangerous. Just ask Siegfried and Roy."

"I'm thinking more of tigers in the wild."

"Not many left, if memory serves," Bolan said.

"They're making a comeback of sorts on Indian game preserves," Brognola told him, "but there's still a thriving trade in pelts and organs."

"Organs?"

"Right. Go figure. In the Eastern culture, certain organs are believed to help male potency."

"I thought that was rhinoceros horn," Bolan said.

"Same thing," Brognola admitted. "Different strokes for different folks."

"So, poachers," Bolan said.

"Big-time. Not only tigers, but elephants, too. Apparently, it's a major crime wave."

"Too bad," the Executioner replied. "But still—"

"I know, it's not our usual."

"Not even close."

"Does the name Balahadra Naraka ring any bells?" Brognola asked.

"Vaguely. Can't place it, though."

"He's a legend of sorts from what I gather," the big Fed explained. "Started out as a small-time poacher, then he caught a prison sentence and escaped, killing some guards as he went. That was ten or twelve years ago, and the government's been hunting him ever since. He's the Indian equivalent of Jesse James or John Dillinger. Naraka has a gang, hooked up with dealers in Calcutta and buyers all over the world. Reports vary, but it seems he's killed at least a hundred game wardens and soldiers. Some reports claim two hundred or more."

"Bad news," Bolan said, "but I still don't see—"

"Our angle?" Brognola had anticipated him. "Last week a U.S. diplomat, one Phillip Langley, paid a visit to West Bengal with his wife. Langley is—or *was*—a member of the President's task force on preservation of endangered species, working in conjunction with the United Nations."

"*Was* a member?" Bolan asked.

"He's dead," Brognola replied. "The wife, too. Some of Naraka's people jumped their convoy on a game preserve ninety miles outside Calcutta. Killed their escorts on the spot, then snatched the Langleys and demanded ransom."

"Washington, of course, refused to pay," Bolan said.

"Right. So, anyway, the army got a lead on where Naraka had them stashed and tried to pull a rescue. When the smoke cleared, they had two dead hostages and one small-timer from the gang, but no sign of Naraka and the rest."

"Which leaves the White House angry and embarrassed," Bolan guessed.

"And shit still rolls downhill," Brognola said. "This load just landed on my doorstep yesterday."

"You want Naraka chastised."

"Neutralized," Brognola said, correcting him. "Along with anybody else who had a hand in murdering the Langleys."

"And the local government can't handle it?"

"They've spent more than a decade chasing him around in circles, getting nowhere. As I mentioned, he's already killed at least a hundred of their officers, and still they haven't laid a glove on him. No reason to suppose they'll score a sudden breakthrough, just because he smoked a couple of Americans."

"A diplomatic squeeze might do the trick," Bolan suggested.

"Some say we're spread too thin as it is, or throwing too much weight around already. Either way, the word's come down to handle it outside normal channels."

"Ah. And where would I start looking if the natives don't know where to find their man?"

"I said they haven't found him," Brognola replied. "That doesn't mean they don't know where he is."

"Collusion?"

"Or ineptitude. It wouldn't be the first time, right?"

"Unfortunately, no," Bolan agreed. "My question's still the same. Where would I start?"

"Calcutta," Brognola suggested. "It's the capital of West Bengal, Naraka's happy hunting ground, and anything he moves to foreign buyers will be passing through the city. I've already tapped the Company for contacts, and they've got a man on standby to assist you if you take the job."

"A native?"

"Born and bred," Brognola said. "He's on the books with a 'reliable' notation."

"Name?"

"I've got his file here," Brognola said, raising his left hand to stroke his overcoat, feeling the fat manila envelope that filled his inside pocket. "And I brought along Naraka's, with some background on the area."

"So, is the White House miffed, or is there some real likelihood this character may pose a future threat?" Bolan asked.

"To the States?" Brognola shrugged. "Who knows? It's not his first kidnapping, just the first involving U.S. citizens. Our analysts are split fifty-fifty, as to whether the experience will scare him off or piss him off so badly that he wants another piece of Uncle Sam."

"It's a distraction from his trade," Bolan remarked.

"Which means he may start taking other risks, making mistakes. I'd hate to see him fixate on the embassy, its personnel. This guy's been living like a hermit in the jungle since his prison break. I'm not sure he was civilized before that all went down, but he's a Grade A wild man now."

"A wild man with a taste for ivory and tigers," Bolan said.

"And hostages. Let's not forget."

"How solid is his dossier?"

"Good question. The ambassador to India says we got everything they have in New Delhi. Beyond that, who knows?"

"Naraka could have someone running interference for him in the government," Bolan suggested.

"It's a possibility, all right."

"And if I find someone like that? What, then?"

"Officially, we'd want to know about it. Off the record, use your own best judgment."

"All right," the warrior said, at last. "Let's see the files."

THE FILES HAD BEEN condensed, photos and all printed on flimsy paper for convenience and easy disposal when Bolan had finished his reading. He sat on a bench in the sunshine, outside Fort McHenry, with Brognola at his side, watching any stray tourist who wandered too close. Bolan read steadily, absorbing all the salient facts and asking questions when he needed to.

His contact, Abhaya Takeri, was a twenty-six-year-old ex-soldier who had dabbled in private security before landing a dull office job in Calcutta. That had lasted for nearly a year before he got restless, picking up covert assignments from his government, and later from the CIA. It wasn't clear in Takeri's case if one hand knew what the other was doing, but he'd managed to avoid any conflicts so far, after three years of service, and that said something for his tradecraft at the very least.

Takeri's photos were a study in contrast. The first, a posed shot in his army uniform, revealed a stern young man who wouldn't smile to save his life, proud of his threads and attitude. The other was a candid shot, taken just as Takeri left a small sidewalk café, his arm around a pretty, laughing young woman. Takeri's smile seemed genuine, good-humored, as if he enjoyed his life. The flimsy printouts meant that Bolan couldn't check the flip side of the photographs for dates, but he assumed the army photo had been taken first. Takeri seemed a little older in the second, definitely more at ease.

Takeri's record in the military had been unremarkable, and most of what he'd done since entering the cloak-and-dagger world was classified. Of course the CIA didn't mind leaking what he'd done for India, as long as it had no impact on his work for the Company. Apparently, Takeri had been used to infiltrate a labor union thought to be involved in sabotage—they weren't, according to his last report—and to disrupt a group of Sikhs who showed displeasure with the government by blowing up department stores. Four bombers had been sent to prison in that case, while their ringleader had committed suicide.

It sounded like a good day's work.

Takeri spoke three languages, had studied martial arts before and after military service, and he'd qualified with standard small arms in the army.

"Sounds all right," Bolan said, handing the dossier to Brognola.

Balahadra Naraka was something else entirely. Thirty-eight years old and a career criminal by anyone's definition, he had survived Calcutta as an orphan, living by theft and his wits on the streets, then fell in with poachers when he was a teenager. The shift to country living didn't help. Naraka was suspected of killing his first game warden at age nineteen, but no charges were filed in that case and he'd remained at large for three more years, then took a fall for shooting tigers. The charge carried a five-year prison sentence, and he'd spent nearly a year in jail prior to trial. Upon conviction, Naraka had received the maximum and was packed off to serve his time.

It took him nearly three years to escape, but he made up for the delay in grisly style. Using a homemade shank, he gutted one guard on the cell block, took another hostage and escaped in one of the prison vehicles. Car and hostage were abandoned on the outskirts of civilization, the guard decapitated, with his head mounted as a hood ornament.

Since then, for nearly twelve years, Balahadra Naraka had been a hunted fugitive, although it barely showed from his lifestyle. Granted, he spent most of his time in tents or tiny jungle villages, but so did half the population of West Bengal. His photos—half a dozen snapped by Naraka's own men and sent to major newspapers—always depicted him in a defiant pose, armed to the teeth, standing beside the carcasses of tigers, elephants, or men in uniform.

Brognola had been right about the bandit-poacher's body count. Although it seemed most of his victims were officials—cops, soldiers, game wardens—no two sources ever quite agreed on how many men he'd killed. The lowest figure Bolan saw, in excerpts from assorted press clippings, was 105; the highest, lifted from a sensational tabloid, ascribed "nearly four hundred" slayings to Naraka and his gang.

It was peculiar, Bolan thought, that no official source kept track of government employees murdered by a bandit on the prowl, but numbers didn't really matter in the last analysis. Naraka was a dangerous opponent, and he'd moved from killing local lawmen to murdering U.S. diplomats.

Bolan assumed the Langley snatch had been a one-time thing, impulsive, maybe even carried out by a subordinate without Naraka's prior knowledge. It made no difference, though, because Naraka had a lifelong pattern of internalizing and repeating bad behavior. If he'd been apprehended for his first known homicide, it might've made a difference. But as it was…

Naraka might be something of a folk hero to rural villagers, who welcomed charity and anyone who helped remove the threat of tigers from their dreary lives, but he still qualified as a mass murderer—perhaps the worst in India since British troops suppressed the *thugee* cult during the nineteenth century. If Bolan could supply the final chapter to Naraka's long and cruel career, so much the better.

"He's a tough one," Bolan told Brognola. "Knows the ground like Jungle Jim. It won't be easy to find him, and even then—"

"You've tackled worse," Brognola said.

"Maybe." Bolan handed back Naraka's file. "Just let me check the ground."

It was the worst of both worlds—first, a teeming city, second largest in the country, steeped in grinding poverty, then swamps and jungles rivaling the thickest, least hospitable on Earth. The Sundarbans, where Bolan would be forced to hunt Naraka if he couldn't catch his target in Calcutta, spanned 2,560 square miles in West Bengal, with more sprawling across the border into Bangladesh. The Indian portion included a 1,550-square-mile game preserve, where three hundred tigers were protected by law, since the early 1970s.

Nor did the Sundarbans consist of any ordinary jungle. Seventy percent of the region lay under salt water, comprising the world's largest mangrove swamp, crisscrossed by hundreds of creeks and tributaries feeding three large rivers—the Brahmaputra, the Ganges and the Meghna. Access to much of the region was boats only, and if tigers missed a visitor on land, the tourist still had to watch out for sharks and salt-water crocodiles. Electrified dummies had failed to discourage the cats, and every tourist party that entered the Sundarbans traveled with armed guards.

All that, *before* poachers and bandits were added to the mix.

"Sounds like malaria country," Bolan said.

"I've got a medic on standby to update your shots," Brognola answered.

"Thoughtful to a fault."

"That's me."

"All right," the Executioner replied. "I'm in."

4

Calcutta

The cab dropped Bolan and Takeri two blocks north of Bolan's hotel and they walked back through the darkness, alert for any sign of followers. Spotting none, they entered the lobby, where the night clerk shot a glance at them, suspicious, then ignored them after recognizing Bolan.

Takeri started toward the creaky elevator, but Bolan stopped him with a word and steered him toward the stairs. If anything had soured since he'd left the place that evening, Bolan didn't want to meet new adversaries for the first time when the elevator's door jerked open and the hostiles blazed away at point-blank range.

It proved to be a wasted effort, if security precautions could be wasted in a combat zone. No enemies were waiting for them on the third floor, none in Bolan's room after he used his key and cleared the threshold in a rush, pistol in hand. The exercise did not make him feel foolish, even so.

Better to be alive and taking too much care than to relax and die.

When they were safely locked inside the room, lights on and curtains drawn, Bolan repeated his original question. "All right, we're off the streets. Now fill me in on who we're running from."

Takeri found a seat and filled it, stretching in an effort to relax. "You understand I cannot be precisely sure. I did not recognize those men."

"Best guess?"

"It was the first direct attempt upon my life since I left military service. I have enemies, of course, but in the circumstances I assume it was related to your mission."

"Break it down."

"Sorry? Oh, yes, I see. In preparation for your coming, I initiated certain contacts. Seeking information on Balahadra Naraka and his associates, attempting to identify his local contacts, vendors and the like. I exercised the utmost caution, but—"

"You tripped some wires, regardless," Bolan finished for him.

"It is possible," Takeri answered ruefully. "The other possibility, revenge for some work previously done, strikes me as too coincidental at the present time."

"Agreed."

It was a poor beginning to the mission, with his guide and contact compromised, already hunted by the enemy. Bolan had been sucked into the violence, seen by the enemy, and might have sacrificed the critical advantage of surprise.

Or, maybe not.

"You need to lay out everything you've done," he told Takeri. "Everyone you've spoken to about Naraka, when and where. If we can figure out who's hunting you, it tells us which direction we should go to minimize exposure."

"Certainly." Takeri frowned. "But, everyone?"

"In order, if you can," Bolan replied. "We've got all night."

"Do we have coffee?"

Bolan made a call to room service, then settled in to listen while they waited for the coffee to arrive.

"I started with police contacts," Takeri said. "A Captain Gupta in Calcutta, who collaborates with agents from the

Ministry of the Interior to curb the traffic in endangered species and their relics."

"Is he straight?" Bolan asked.

"Meaning honest?"

"That's my meaning."

"I believe so," Takeri said. "His promotion came through merit, based on his arrests of poachers and their contacts in the export trade. Over the past three years, he has maintained an average of three arrests per week."

"How many were convicted?" Bolan asked.

Takeri shrugged at that. "I've no idea. Is it important that we know?"

"Where I come from," Bolan replied, "it's not unusual for crooked cops to make a lot of busywork arrests that go nowhere. They pick up prostitutes and small-time dealers, run them through the system to compile a quota of arrests and bag their commendations, while the courts dish out probation and small fines. Meanwhile, the cops draw paychecks from both sides, and business continues as usual."

"I see," Takeri said. "Of course we have such officers in India, as well. But I do not think that Gupta stands among them."

"Based on what?"

"His reputation. While I've told you his promotion came through merit, I should first have mentioned that it had been long delayed, apparently by his refusal to participate in—what is the expression? Office politics?"

Bolan felt better. "Okay, then. What did he give you?"

"Names and addresses of dealers known or thought to traffic in the sort of merchandise Naraka normally supplies. You understand that it is not all tiger pelts and ivory?"

"I got the briefing," Bolan said. "Weird mumbo-jumbo medicine."

"To you and I, of course," Takeri answered. "But to millions in the East, such items are believed to be extremely potent—as their purchasers would hope to be. The so-called medicine concocted from these outlawed items has been used throughout Asia for several thousand years."

"And no one's noticed that it isn't working?" Bolan asked.

"Perhaps it *does* work, Mr. Cooper, for selected devotees. In the Caribbean and parts of the United States, you have practitioners of voodoo, yes?"

"That's right."

"In Africa and parts of South America, cults practice human sacrifice this very day."

"I wouldn't rule it out," Bolan replied.

"Belief," Takeri said. "It has great power, even though skeptics deny it. When your faith healers perform on television, many people laugh, dismiss it as a fraud, and change the channel, yes? But millions more *believe*. And who's to say that none is truly healed?"

"All right," Bolan said, "let's assume that eating tiger organs makes some old man happy in the sack. I wasn't sent to analyze folk medicine or magic. Let's cut to the chase."

"I am attempting to explain," Takeri said, "that some of those with whom Naraka deals are men of faith. They'll never give him up. I have a list of six or seven names but have not pressed them, knowing it would be a waste of time."

"Who have you pressed?" Bolan asked.

"I made inquiries with two dealers in Calcutta whom Captain Gupta identified as covert traffickers in tiger pelts and ivory. Posing as a potential buyer, I approached them and was courteously told that while such items sometimes come on offer from the hinterlands, it is illegal to purchase or sell them. The problem, I suspect, lies in the fact that I am native to the area, while nearly all the traffic in such items flows to foreign dealers."

"So, you struck out with the vendors," Bolan said.

"Correct."

"And underneath that courtesy, did either one of them smell like a murderer?"

"In my assessment, no."

"We're getting nowhere," Bolan said.

"I must confess some disappointment in my progress, to that point," Takeri admitted. "But I did not grow discouraged. If the dealers would not speak to me, I thought, perhaps I could get through to someone else."

"Such as?"

"Illicit trade of any kind requires protection. Captain Gupta let me have another name."

"I'm listening," the Executioner replied.

Takeri studied the American, impressed by his intensity, his bearing and the way he had performed during their skirmish with the assassins on the street. The man who called himself Matt Cooper seemed a worthy ally, and the CIA was paying for Takeri's services—but it was still a risky business, as had recently been demonstrated by the rude attempt upon his life.

"Girish Vyasa," he replied after a moment's hesitation. "He is a customs agent. As you know, cooperation from the Customs Service is essential to the foreign trade in contraband."

"Of course," Bolan agreed.

"Girish Vyasa is a man of certain appetites, the cost of which exceed his salary. Perhaps they also make him vulnerable to extortion. Who can say? In any case, Naraka pays him handsomely for letting certain shipments pass without detailed inspection. Others may be paying him, as well."

"Why is Vyasa still in business if your Captain Gupta knows all this?" Bolan asked.

"It seems that Vyasa in turn is protected by men of influence in Calcutta and New Delhi. Corruption spreads. No government is perfectly immune."

Nodding, Bolan replied, "I take it you inquired about Vyasa in more detail?"

"Certainly. And therein lies my fault, presumably. He is, as I've explained, protected—both officially and unofficially."

"Someone got wise and put the hunters on your trail."

"I must assume that is the case," Takeri said. "If any negligence of mine has jeopardized your mission, I must now apologize."

"We couldn't count on cover all the way," Bolan replied. "I would've liked a better lead, but we can work with this."

Takeri frowned. "But if the hunters, as you put it, are aware of our intentions—"

"Scratch that," Bolan interrupted. "We'll assume they're onto you for asking questions, but they won't know why, or who you're working for. They don't know me at all, beyond a glimpse tonight, and there's no way they have a handle on my plans."

"Because?"

"I haven't made plans, yet."

Takeri's frown deepened. "I draw no reassurance from that statement, Mr. Cooper."

Bolan shrugged. "Don't sweat it. Coming in, I had no fix on the best way to reach Naraka. Now I'm warming up to it."

"You have a plan, in fact?"

"It's coming to me. First, I need to have a word with this Vyasa character."

"I say again, he is protected."

"Not from me."

The cutting edge of Bolan's tone sent an unexpected chill rippling along Takeri's spine.

"You would approach him directly?"

"That's right."

"And if he's being watched? Guarded?"

"We'll have to take that chance."

Takeri's frown deepened. "When you say 'we'—"

"You'll need to show me where Vyasa lives and point him

out. Aside from that, I'll need details of what your Captain Gupta has on him, what links him to Naraka. Dates, facts, figures. Anything at all to crack him open, make him feel cooperative."

"I see." From where Takeri sat, it was a grim vision indeed. "But once again I ask, if he is guarded?"

"We'll see how it goes," Bolan replied. "You did okay tonight against those cutters."

"Still, if you had not arrived just when you did, the outcome may have been a disappointment."

"We'll avoid that in the future if we can."

"If I am permitted to inquire, what *are* you, Mr. Cooper? Surely not an analyst."

"I wouldn't say that. No."

"What, then?"

"A trouble-shooter," the American replied. "We'll let it go at that, if you don't mind."

"Of course."

"About those details on Vyasa—"

"Captain Gupta did not favor me with all specifics of the case, you understand."

"Just give me what you have."

"On several occasions—five or six, I think he said—Vyasa has been seen with export dealers linked to the Naraka group. In normal circumstances, these are men Vyasa should have been investigating, possibly arresting, but he seemed to be on cordial terms with all of them. At two meetings, police observed the passage of an envelope into Vyasa's hands."

"Containing money?" Bolan asked.

Takeri shrugged. "Sadly, they did not stop him to inquire. There is a mystery of sorts in that respect. His bank accounts—those known to the authorities, at least—show no unusual or unexplained deposits, yet Vyasa lives beyond his means."

"So, he's been hiding cash somewhere."

"Presumably."

"Maybe we'll shake some of it loose from him and use it on the next phase of our journey."

"Which would be?"

"I thought you understood. I'm here to find Naraka."

"But he almost never leaves the Sundarbans."

"I guess that's where we'll find him, then," Bolan stated.

Again, the deadly *we*, Takeri thought. "I should advise you, Mr. Cooper, that my personal experience in fieldwork of this sort is...limited."

"You spent time in the military, I believe?"

Takeri masked his first rush of surprise. "That's true."

"And you're my guide for the duration, yes?"

"Correct." Takeri felt the noose settle around his neck.

"No problem, then."

No problem. The phrase was said as if the words would not only allay Takeri's fear but turn him into something he was not. A hunting guide, perhaps. A jungle warrior. True, he *had* been trained for living off the land and fighting in the wilderness, but all of that seemed long ago and far away.

"I will endeavor not to fail you, Mr. Cooper," he replied.

"It's Matt. And failure's not an option."

"This is all to do with the Americans, I take it? Those Naraka kidnapped?"

"Those he killed. That's right."

"If he had not involved your people—"

"Then I likely wouldn't be here. But he did, I am and we're together in this thing for better or worse, if you think you can handle it."

Takeri knew he should resist the challenge, not rise to the bait, but at the moment it seemed irresistible. "I can. I will."

"Good man. Now, what say you go on and bring me up to speed about Vyasa. I'd like to drop in for a visit tonight, and before we do that I need chapter and verse."

Takeri had a sense that everything was happening too rapidly, that he was being swept away, but what choice did he have? His working contract with the CIA demanded full cooperation, and he'd gone so far already in the matter that his life was placed in jeopardy. Those who had tried to kill him would already have his home staked out. At least, with the American, he had a better fighting chance.

But the Sundarbans!

"All right," Takeri said at last.

5

As they discussed their short-range plans, the Executioner took stock of Abhaya Takeri, comparing his reticence to the forceful response he'd witnessed from Takeri in the street a short time earlier.

The change was only natural, of course. When Bolan met the Indian, Takeri had been fighting for his life, with no time to reflect on the advisability of any certain move. A kill-or-be-killed situation always tested humans to the limit. Those who passed the test survived, while those who failed were meat for the machine.

During the street assault, Takeri's military training and survival instincts had emerged to save him, with some timely help from Bolan. Whether he would have survived alone was something else, a question left unanswered for all time, but it was clear to Bolan that Takeri had the courage, strength and will to fight if motivated properly.

Sitting in the relative security of Bolan's hotel room, Takeri had a chance to think about what he was getting into, weigh the odds against him, letting worms of doubt nibble at his resolve. He wasn't balking yet, but Bolan knew it could happen.

Strong men could defeat themselves before a contest started by exaggerating the prospective difficulties in their minds. Some heroes, Bolan realized, were simply men who had no time to stop and think.

What soldier started his day with plans to fall on top of a grenade? Or charge the muzzle-blast of an emplaced machine gun, armed with nothing but a satchel charge? Who got up in the morning, thinking, *Man, I'd love to die today?*

Bolan recognized Takeri's hesitancy and sympathized with it, but he couldn't afford an ally who balked when the going got tough. A guide was no use if he brought up the rear.

Bolan went briskly through the plan, watching Takeri sketch a floor plan of Girish Vyasa's large apartment house. The layout of his living space would be a mystery until they crossed the threshold, but Takeri had spotted exits, elevators, where the doorman stood, which entrances were normally unwatched.

"You've thought this through," Bolan observed.

"I guessed it might be necessary to approach him," Takeri said, "but I had no plans to go inside myself."

"Plans change. Go with the flow."

The smile was thin. "I'll do my best."

"He doesn't have security? No bodyguards?"

Takeri shook his head. "Nothing like that. Vyasa is—or claims to be—simply a public servant. Who would wish to harm him?"

"Good," Bolan replied. "That makes it easier."

He spread a large map of Calcutta on the bed, smoothing its creases with his hand, and said, "Let's plot the route and find at least one alternative in case we have to bail."

Takeri bent over the map, peering closely at it, finally bringing an index finger to rest on the glossy paper. "We are here," he told Bolan, "and Vyasa lives…here."

A maze of streets some two miles wide separated Bolan's hotel from his target. One major street cut through the heart of it, a virtual straight-line approach with minor jogs at either end. Bolan memorized the street names, thankful most of them were printed on the map in English. Then, having accomplished that, he set about selecting paths of possible retreat.

He didn't plan to fail but knew it was always possible. They might be intercepted prior to reaching Vyasa's apartment—by police, an unexpected bodyguard, more of the thugs who'd tried to kill Takeri earlier—and so have to abort the mission. Even at the threshold or beyond, security devices might compel a hasty exit from Vyasa's eighth-floor flat. In that case, they'd be glad to have escape routes plotted, memorized, ready to use.

Calcutta's teeming streets could be a help, then, if they had to fight or run. A help…or just a maze, where all roads led to death.

Bolan spent time tracing the streets, burning that section of the map into his memory. Takeri indicated certain one-way streets, others where foot traffic made passage slow or even dangerous in darkness. The nearest police substation was fifteen minutes from Vyasa's apartment under normal nighttime driving conditions.

Bolan listened and absorbed the information, hoping it would serve him well. He needed information from Girish Vyasa, but there was a limit to his need. He wouldn't jeopardize the innocent, and he wouldn't fire on police officers doing their duty.

Bolan had bruised his share of lawmen, frightened some, and even helped to put a few in prison—but he wouldn't kill an honest cop to save his own life, or Takeri's.

A crooked customs agent, though, was a different story.

When he was finished charting streets, Bolan turned to Takeri once again and said, "Give me the rundown on Vyasa."

"Rundown?"

"What's he like? Describe him physically, his habits, anything you have. Fill in the blanks."

"Of course." Takeri closed his eyes briefly, as if reviewing data tattooed on the inside of his eyelids, then began. "He has a birthday in October, at which time he will be forty-two years old. He is five feet and seven inches tall, weighing 150 pounds. He has a small tattoo—"

"I'll recognize him," Bolan interrupted. "What about the rest?"

"His customs personnel file will not have the information you require," Takeri said, "but Captain Gupta and my private observations may, as you say, fill the blanks."

"I'm listening."

"Vyasa is a lifelong bachelor. Women apparently hold no attraction for him. He prefers…young men."

"I take it that's still frowned upon in India?" Bolan asked.

"Most assuredly. It is a fact of life, perhaps, but still repressed. There is no movement here, as in America, to bring homosexuals out of the cupboard."

"Closet," Bolan corrected him.

"Sorry?"

"It's not important. Go ahead."

"Vyasa's lifestyle has not been exposed. He would. be driven from his public office if that were the case."

"But Captain Gupta knows?"

"Of course."

"So, why not play that card and flush him out if he's regarded as corrupt?"

"Again, there is the matter of protection. Captain Gupta might succeed in ruining Vyasa's reputation, but his own would also suffer."

"From the backlash?" When Takeri only stared and frowned, Bolan revised his choice of terms. "Reprisals."

"Ah. Exactly so. He might not be dismissed, you understand, but there are other ways to force him out. Transfers, official reprimands, demotions based on petty incidents."

"Bureaucracy," Bolan replied.

"The very thing."

It was the same in every nation, Bolan supposed. Benedict

Arnold had been driven to betray America, at least in part, by petty bureaucratic slights that kept him from promotion in the Continental Army. Every government employee had at least one tale of persecution to relate.

"You think Naraka may have used Vyasa's sex life to control him?"

"With the money, which Vyasa obviously craves," Takeri said, "it is a possibility."

"Okay," Bolan replied. "Let's go and see the man."

BOLAN'S RENTAL CAR was a four-door Skoda Octavia, a mid-size Indian model in silver that looked more like battleship gray. Before leaving the hotel room, he took the Steyr AUG from its hiding place, assembled it and stowed it in a nylon tote.

Takeri watched Bolan sling the bag over his shoulder, then inquired, "Are we going to war?"

"You never know," Bolan said. "Better safe than sorry."

Takeri's expression suggested that he was sorry already, but he made no comment as they rode the elevator down and crossed the lobby, turning left and passing through a narrow alley to the hotel's small, fenced parking lot. A middle-aged attendant dressed in what appeared to be a Boy Scout uniform examined Bolan's key, then wheeled the gate open and waved them out into the sultry night.

Bolan had left the city map behind, trusting his memory and good sense of direction to convey him through the streets. Calcutta was a crowded, often wretched city, but it was a city nonetheless. Bolan was not intimidated by its architecture, slums or residents. His focus on the mission didn't leave him any time to dwell on the affluence or poverty surrounding him.

The drive, some two miles and a quarter, took the better part of twenty minutes, with repeated stops for traffic lights, pedestrians, rickshaws and beggars in the street. Police were not in evidence along the route, and Bolan guessed they were spread thin across the city, drawn away from traffic duty for the most part by incessant small emergencies.

Calcutta had a reputation, dating from colonial times—the infamous "Black Hole" incident that claimed British lives in 1756—to modern acts of terrorism by the United Liberation Front of Assam. Religious, caste and tribal conflicts had inflated the local death toll over time, while random murders during rapes and robberies were downplayed by the local press. Rumors of human sacrifice to Kali still persisted from Calcutta and environs, though the case had not been proved in court. Bolan had had his own experience with Kali, and it was something he'd never forget. It was impossible to calculate the missing-person statistics, when no one really knew how many people occupied the city on a given day.

How many would be dead or missing in the morning, thanks to Bolan? He could not predict a tally, hoped that he would not be forced to kill that night, but at a certain point the choice would be taken from his hands. Girish Vyasa would decide whether to balk or to cooperate. If there were watchers at his flat, unnoticed by Takeri, yet another element of risk came into play.

No matter where he went within the city, or in India at large, Bolan would stand out in the crowd. He couldn't pass for native, and while U.S.-European types were not entirely strangers to the region, those encountered by the natives on a daily basis were predominately businessmen or tourists, with a smattering of diplomats thrown in. Bolan might pass for a tourist at first glance, but closer examination quickly gave the lie to that facade.

This night, the darkness was his friend and Abhaya Takeri was his guide. His target was a man he'd never met, who might not live to see another sunrise. Come what may, Bolan had work to do, and he would not allow himself to be diverted from the job at hand.

An ambulance came up behind them, weaving awkwardly through traffic with its siren warbling. Bolan didn't know if it was racing to an accident or toward a hospital, already bearing victims of some private tragedy, but he slowed to let it pass. Most of the other drivers, whether on four wheels or two, clung stubbornly to their appointed lanes.

Beside him, in the shotgun seat, Bolan noticed Takeri's sharp attention to the ambulance. No mind reader, he still had an idea of what was happening inside his contact's head. Takeri was unsettled, naturally, by the effort to assassinate him, that anxiety exacerbated by their mission to accost Vyasa at his home. Given a choice, Takeri might have bought a ticket on the next train out of town for parts unknown, but he was sticking to the job.

So far.

Trust was a rare commodity in Bolan's world, bestowed on those who earned it under fire. Takeri hadn't reached that level yet, though Bolan read him as a decent man whose sense of duty kept him for the most part on the straight and narrow path.

What would he do the next time they were challenged, threatened, placed in danger?

Only time would tell.

Bolan spotted the number of Vyasa's drab apartment house just as Takeri said, "This is the place." He drove past and boxed the block at a crawl, scanning sidewalks for any lookouts who might be stationed among the passersby or street corner beggars. None was obvious, and so he started looking for a parking place.

In such a crowded city, space was at a premium. Curbside parking was out of the question, and the underground garage beneath Vyasa's place required a card for passage through the roll-down gate. Reluctantly, Bolan settled for a public garage a half block farther east, taking a ticket from a stern attendant dressed in olive drab.

Using the park-and-pay garage would slow them, coming and going, but he didn't feel like handing Takeri the keys and having him circle aimlessly while Bolan went upstairs alone. He didn't think Takeri would bug out on him, but he was already a hunted man, and with the Steyr in the rental car it was a recipe for potential disaster.

Bolan found a spot on the garage's third level, nosed into it and killed the engine. Unhappy with the choice, he left the Steyr in its bag, locked in the trunk.

Takeri frowned as they stepped out, and asked him, "What about the other item?"

"Circumstances alter cases," Bolan said. "I'll go with what I'm carrying."

"Which is?"

"Enough to get us by, with any luck. Ready?"

Takeri shrugged. "I think the proper answer is, as ready as I'll ever be."

"Okay," Bolan replied. "Let's hope that's good enough."

6

Unlike so many apartment houses in the United States, most of those in Calcutta did not bear names intended to evoke thoughts of woodlands or beaches, meadows or glens. Instead, they were conspicuously numbered, large block numerals posted for the convenience of visitors, deliverymen and emergency workers.

The block that Girish Vyasa called home was number 4539. Its gray hue varied slightly from that of its neighbors, giving the block a mottled look, but otherwise Bolan saw nothing to distinguish it from any other building on the street. As he approached the service entrance with Takeri on his heels, he stayed alert for sentries and discovered none except the guard employed by management to watch the door and alleyway.

Unlike the doorman posted out front, this watchman didn't have a uniform. Instead, he wore a laminated tag on his lapel, bearing a photo with a vaguely stunned expression on his face and several lines of text that Bolan couldn't read. The small man stiffened to a rough approximation of attention as they neared his post, bracing himself for confrontation with the strangers on his turf.

Takeri handled it, fishing inside one of his pockets to produce a card, which he displayed to the watchman while speaking rapidly in Hindi. Bolan didn't understand a word of it, but it produced results. The alley lookout ducked his head, nodded respectfully and stood with eyes averted while he held the door for them to enter.

"What was that?" Bolan asked, as the door shut behind them.

With a smile, Takeri answered, "In Calcutta I wear—what is the expression? Many hats? Today I am a state building inspector, sadly forced to show a foreign architect around the city, briefing him on rules and regulations of construction."

"That's not bad."

Takeri shrugged. "There is a risk he will remember us, but if there's trouble when we leave, his first thought will be self-protection. I expect that he would lie about admitting us and claim that no one passed his door."

"Sounds good to me," Bolan replied.

Inside, the place was cleaner than Bolan had expected. There'd been no graffiti on the outer walls, and now he saw the service area was well maintained, if not precisely spick-and-span. They passed a bank of washer-dryers stacked against one wall, to face the choice of stairs or service elevator.

"Do we ride or climb?" Takeri asked.

"We climb," Bolan said, voting on the side of caution once again.

Eight floors meant sixteen flights of concrete stairs, their footsteps echoing along the way. Bolan paused at each landing to listen and peer through the small windows in the numbered access doors, eyeing bland corridors through a sandwich of wire mesh and high-impact glass. He tested each doorknob in turn and found them all unlocked, doubtless for safety purposes in case of fire or some other emergency.

They passed no one along the way, ascending quietly until they reached the seventh floor. As Bolan turned back from the door's small window, Takeri took a risk and caught him by the sleeve.

"Problem?"

"I have not asked what you intend to do," Takeri said.

"We covered this. I need more intel on Vyasa's dealings with Naraka. How they stay in touch, where we can find Naraka—anything Vyasa knows."

"And if he does not wish to speak?"

"I'll try persuading him," Bolan replied.

"With that?" Takeri nodded toward the slight bulge under Bolan's jacket, at the left armpit. The subtle outline of his holstered Glock.

"If necessary," Bolan said.

"And will you kill him?"

Bolan felt and instantly suppressed a flash of irritation. They were wasting time.

"I thought you understood the mission," he replied. "I'm shutting down Naraka's operation, one way or another. Are we clear?"

"I've never killed a man before," Takeri said.

"With any luck at all, this time tomorrow you can say the same. Right now, time's running short, and I can't send you back alone, past Mr. Nosy on the door downstairs."

"I understand. But if there should be difficulties, I am not prepared. I have no weapon."

Bolan felt a small measure of relief. "Just do your best," he answered. "Pick up what you can. Main thing—avoid my line of fire."

Takeri nodded solemnly. "Of course."

"Now, if we're done?"

"We are."

Bolan took more care on the last two flights of stairs, planting his feet precisely, minimizing noise along the way. Takeri followed, mimicking his caution. At the eighth floor's access door, Bolan edged close enough to check the window, first a glance and then a longer searching look.

"No watchdogs I can see from here," he told Takeri, "but that doesn't mean we're clear."

"If you suspect a trap—"

"I don't," Bolan said. "But you need to be prepared in case. I go in first. If something happens, head downstairs as fast as you can go. Don't wait for me."

"And then?"

"If I'm not right behind you, hit the bricks. Forget about the car and go on foot."

"Go where?" Takeri asked.

"Away. Wherever you feel safe. If I'm not with you when you hit the street, odds are you've seen the last of me. Take care of number one."

"But—"

"Let's just get this done, all right?"

"Yes. Certainly."

Bolan left his pistol holstered as he turned the doorknob, pulled the door toward him and stepped across the threshold. He could feel Takeri at his back, a nervous shadow, ready to advance or flee, depending on what happened in the next few seconds.

Which was nothing.

If Vyasa had bodyguards unknown to Takeri, they weren't stationed in the hallway outside his apartment. Downstairs in the lobby, perhaps? If so, they had already missed their chance to intercept intruders.

"Ready?" Bolan asked.

"Ready," Takeri said.

Bolan moved toward Vyasa's door, then froze as it swung open, light and angry voices spilling through its frame, into the corridor.

"Get back!" he whispered, and rushed Takeri toward the service stairs.

IT STARTED AS A CHILDISH lovers' quarrel. Girish Vyasa had emerged from the bathroom to find his partner of the moment

—a nineteen-year-old dream named Chandra Vasin—sifting through his collection of carefully alphabetized CDs, pulling out disks at random, replacing them haphazardly. Still hot and dripping from the shower, standing with a bath towel wrapped around his waist like a sarong, the sight immediately irritated him.

"Chandra?"

"Mmm-hmm?" Still focused on the CD in his hand, not even glancing up in common courtesy.

"Please pay attention, Chandra."

"What?" That damned, infuriating whine.

"I've asked you several times to pay attention and replace the CDs in their proper order."

"Proper order." Now the boy was mocking him. "It's only music, Gir. The disks don't have to be just so."

Vyasa felt the angry color rising in his cheeks, fresh heat entirely unrelated to his recent steaming shower. "Please correct me if I am mistaken, Chandra. Are the disks not mine?"

"You *know* they are."

"Then I should be allowed to say if there's a proper order, yes?"

The young man muttered something under his breath, turning away.

"I didn't hear that," Vyasa said.

"So?"

"Repeat it, please."

"I said, if you insist."

"I *do* insist. Is that a problem?"

"If you must know, Gir, I think it's foolish."

Anger turned a corner, surging toward the straightaway that led to fury. "Do you, now?"

"You asked. I answered you. What of it, Gir?"

"You constantly surprise me, Chandra."

"Yes?"

"Indeed. I make you welcome in my home, show you affection, buy you gifts. Ask nothing in return—"

"Nothing?" That mocking smile again, the one that always made Vyasa want to slap it from his lover's face.

"And still, you seek out new ways to insult me."

"I was looking at the CDs, Gir. You make a crisis out of nothing."

"Your disrespect must count for something, surely, Chandra. Otherwise, why make such a production of it?"

"Disrespect?"

"For me, my home and my belongings," Vyasa said. "I begin to wonder why you visit me at all."

"When you're like this, I wonder, too," Chandra replied.

"When I'm *like this?* Explain yourself!"

"Obsessing over every little thing, as if it meant the world. I never know if you've been scolded by your boss at work, or if you're simply in a rotten mood, but you can be a bitch sometimes."

"Can I?"

"You asked."

"Are we enumerating faults tonight?"

A taunting shrug from Chandra. "If you ask a question and I do not answer, then you're angry. When I answer, it gets worse."

Vyasa crossed the living room, no longer conscious of his partial nudity, the damp towel wrapped around his waist. Anger possessed him, even as a small part of his mind stood off to one side, watching the pathetic scene unfold with perfect apathy.

"Why should the simple truth provoke my anger, Chandra? I appreciate it. It permits me to express myself in kind."

"Please do."

"I've meant to tell you for some time, exactly what a lazy, snide, ungrateful whelp you are. The simple truth, my dear."

"You've never found me lazy when it matters, Gir. As for ungrateful...well, perhaps I'm simply getting tired."

"Of what?"

"The games you play. All generous and sweet one moment, cheap and cruel the next. I wonder, sometimes, if you're not two people stuck in the same body, fighting for control. The lover and the bitch."

"Don't call me that again," Vyasa ordered.

"Lover?"

"It is a mistake for you to test me, Chandra."

"This nonsense with CDs is exactly what I mean," the youth pressed on. "Who cares if one stands to the left or right of any other on the shelf? You've had them all forever. You can recognize the labels when you see them. Why make such a fuss?"

"It is a matter of convenience," Vyasa said.

"It's a demonstration of *control.* You always have to run things, don't you, Gir? Controlling what we eat and watch on television, what I wear, the way we—"

"*This* is what I mean about your damned ingratitude," Vyasa snapped. "I give you everything a person could want, and still you—"

"Everything? I don't think so."

"What are you lacking, then?"

"Parties. My friends. *My life.*"

"Your life? Was it so wonderful before we met? I found you on the street, Chandra."

"And you remind me of it every day."

"To help you realize how far you've come. It could be worse, you know."

"I wonder, sometimes."

"Do you?" Fuming, Vyasa clenched his fists.

"Sometimes, when I forget to place the records *properly.*"

As he pronounced the word, making an insult of it, Chandra turned and flung the CD that he held across Vyasa's living room. It sailed beyond the couch and struck the farthest wall, its plastic case exploding, while the bright disk plummeted from view.

"You spiteful brat!"

"Old bitch!"

Vyasa lashed out with his right hand, aimed an openhanded slap at Chandra's face, but Chandra saw it coming and retreated, dodging out of range. He cursed Vyasa in Hindi, railing at his ancestors three generations gone. Vyasa lunged again, with a clenched fist this time, but Chandra was too fast for him. A mocking laugh exploded from the young man's lips as he ducked toward the shelf filled with CDs, thrust out a slender arm and swept it clean.

"Oh no!" he jeered. "They're all *mixed up!* Whatever shall we do!"

Vyasa rushed him then, aware after the third stride that he'd lost his towel. That brought a whoop of laughter from the bobbing, weaving youth.

"It's such a tiny thing," he said with a sneer. "Put it away, old man. No need for that, with me."

Vyasa chased Chandra around the room, caroming off furniture that bruised his hips and legs, spewing a stream of insults and obscenities that seemed to erupt from some bottomless cistern of malice inside him. Clutching fingers fell short of Chandra each time he lunged, while Chandra jeered and mocked him, taunting him with crude gestures.

As always, it came down to this. Flirtation and pursuit gave way to blissful happiness, but only for a fleeting time. No matter who Vyasa chose as the object of his affection, there was always some flaw, some defect that became more repulsive as time slipped away. Soon, Vyasa grew irritable, then spiteful, finally erupting into fury over one last insult, small or large.

In his quiet, rational moments, Vyasa sometimes wondered if the problem lay with him, rather than his companions, but he couldn't face the rest of his interminable life if that were true. Better to blame the young ones than the old dog who was long past learning any further tricks.

At some point in their manic chase, Chandra grabbed Vyasa's fallen towel and started snapping at him with it, flicking first toward his pursuer's face, then toward his flopping genitals and back again. The giggling mockery fueled Vyasa's rage to the point where he snatched up a lamp, brandished it overhead, and sprinted after Chandra with his awkward bludgeon raised on high—until he reached the end of its short cord and it was snatched back from his grasp, shattering on impact with the floor.

Chandra's delighted giggles sputtered off to nothing as he saw the murderous expression on Vyasa's face. At once, the youth knew that he'd pushed the game too far, and he was running out of time. When Vyasa snarled and resumed his pursuit, instead of leading him on another chase around the room's plush furnishings, Chandra bolted in a beeline for the door.

He reached it seconds ahead of his host, risked a jeer in parting as Vyasa cursed him, then Vyasa slammed the door and slumped against it. He felt wasted, nearly broken, on the verge of bitter tears.

Another soul mate gone, just when he'd managed to persuade himself that Chandra was the true and only one.

What if there *was* no true one?

That bitter thought skewered Girish Vyasa like a knife between his ribs. Sniffling, he turned, retrieved his towel and held it limp in one hand as he started toward his lonely bedroom.

A muffled rapping on the door surprised him.

Could it be Chandra returning to apologize? Had the young man already recognized his error and come back to make amends?

Giddy with hope, Vyasa threw the towel around his waist, clutching it tight with one hand, while his other found and turned the doorknob. "Chandra, I—"

Two strangers stood before him, one of them a tall white man, aiming a pistol at Vyasa's face.

"Be calm," the armed man said. "Play nice, and you might stay alive."

7

Takeri found himself redundant as a translator. Vyasa, as a senior customs agent, was fluent in both Hindi and English. Takeri wished he had remained outside—or, better yet, at home—but it was too late to rewrite history.

The scene's most startling aspect was Vyasa himself, a reed-slender man, nearly nude but for the bath towel clutched around his waist with one white-knuckled hand. Behind him, on the floor, a pricey lamp lay broken, but four others in the room provided ample light for Takeri to read the fear on Vyasa's face.

"Who are you?" he managed to ask. "What do you want?"

"Sit down," Bolan instructed him. The pistol in his hand wagged toward the nearby sofa.

"But—"

"Sit first. Then talk."

"I should get dressed."

"You're fine." Another waggle of the pistol, toward the couch. "Just sit."

Vyasa did as he was told, careful to keep the makeshift skirt in place as he sat.

"Now," Vyasa said, "if I may ask—"

"I'll ask," Bolan said, interrupting him. "You answer. If you're honest and you have the information we require, maybe you'll live."

"Maybe?" Vyasa's voice, already high-pitched, had acquired a breathless tone.

"Consider it a challenge," Bolan said. "Ready to start?"

Vyasa blinked at each man in turn, then nodded.

"Good. We're looking for a friend of yours," Bolan explained. "Balahadra Naraka. Since the pair of you are such good chums—"

"You've made a serious mistake," Vyasa protested. "Naraka is a criminal."

"And so are you," Bolan replied. "We know about the bribes, all right? Your cloak-and-dagger repertoire could use an overhaul. We're not here to debate the facts."

"But I—"

The pistol stopped him, Bolan leaning in to place its muzzle on the round tip of Girish Vyasa's nose. The small, half-naked man went cross-eyed, staring at it, waiting for the blast that would obliterate his face.

"You need to listen carefully," Bolan said. "We are not policemen. You are not under arrest. Nothing you tell us will be coming back to haunt you in a courtroom. That's the good news. On the other hand, if you can't help us, well, I really don't see any point in keeping you alive. You're just another grubby little thief who violates his oath of office every day, for money. If we throw you out your bedroom window, what's the loss?"

Vyasa suddenly deflated, slumped into the deep cushions surrounding him. Takeri saw that any hope the customs agent might've entertained, whatever chance of pleading innocent, had slithered through his trembling fingers and was gone.

"You wish to know about Naraka? I have met him only once," Vyasa said. "It was almost two years ago. Since then, I deal with his appointed representatives on one hand, export merchants on the other. If you know all this without my help—"

"You're not a stupid man," Bolan said. "I don't see you taking cash from anyone who wanders in and makes a pitch. You'd want to keep a sharp eye on the operation, from a distance, and make sure it's running smoothly. In a pinch, you'd also want a handle on Naraka, just in case you're cornered and you need to make a deal. Like now."

"You flatter me," Vyasa said. "I really don't deserve such credit as a mastermind."

"Too bad," Bolan said, stepping back a pace and leveling his weapon at Vyasa's face.

Then, to Takeri at his side, he said, "At least the only thing we've wasted is a bullet and a little time."

Takeri saw the trigger finger tighten, closed his eyes and waited for the shot, but then Vyasa blurted out, "No! Wait! I'm sorry! I can help!"

"So, help," Bolan replied.

Raising both hands in front of him, as if in prayer, Vyasa said, "You must believe that I don't know *exactly* where Naraka is. He's constantly in motion, hiding from the soldiers and police, but I can place you close to him. That much, I certainly can do."

Bolan glanced at Takeri, cocked an eyebrow as if asking whether it was worth the time and trouble. They could kill Vyasa, his expression seemed to say, and find another source of information elsewhere.

"Honestly!" Vyasa whined. "I swear! Within a few miles, at most. He moves, but never travels very far."

"You have a map around this place?" Bolan inquired.

"A map? Yes, many maps. I'll fetch them."

Rising from the couch, Vyasa momentarily forgot about his towel. Recovering his wits and modesty, he clasped the towel and scurried toward an ornate cabinet that filled one corner of the room. Bolan was close behind him, pistol at the ready, while Takeri trailed them both.

"Nothing but maps," Bolan advised Vyasa. "If you've got a weapon stashed there, it's the worst idea you've had all day."

Vyasa stared at them, bug-eyed, seeming amazed by the idea. "No weapons!" he assured them. "No, sir. Maps of West Bengal. The Sundarbans."

Vyasa opened a drawer one-handed, rummaged inside it and stepped back clutching a stack of folded maps. Returning to the sofa, he placed them on the low-slung coffee table, spent a moment knotting his towel at one hip, then sat and began to sort through the maps. A moment later, he had one spread before them, index finger wandering across a maze of green and blue—the coastal mangrove swamps.

"Naraka hides in here," Vyasa said. "He shifts from place to place, staying a few nights here and there, but nearly always in this area. It is his sanctuary. When he leaves to hunt the elephants and tigers, always he returns to safety here."

"Make me believe you," Bolan said.

Bolan could read the desperation on Vyasa's face. He thought the customs man was playing straight, but there was nothing to be lost by piling on a little extra pressure. Making sure.

"It's true, I swear!" Vyasa said. "The time I met him, when he sent for me, two of his men met me at Diamond Harbour…here." A bony finger jabbed the map. "They had a boat. We followed one of these small rivers to reach a camp approximately…there."

"How long ago was that?" Bolan asked.

"Something over two years. Twenty-seven months, I think."

"That's a long time," Bolan observed.

"Yes, sir. But I ask questions when I speak to those who buy the ivory, the tiger pelts and other things. They know Naraka well and trust me since I—"

"You sold your soul," Bolan suggested.

"They have no reason to fear me," Vyasa said. "I am casual, not pressing them. In passing, when they talk about the hunts, I ask them where Naraka stays. They tell me here and there, another place each time, but always in this area." Vyasa's finger drew a circle on the map, encompassing roughly three hundred square miles.

"That doesn't really pin it down," Bolan told Vyasa.

"What more can I say? Do you want me to lie?"

"This isn't worth your life," Bolan replied. His pistol rose toward target acquisition.

"Wait!" A lonely tear spilled from Vyasa's left eye, rolling down his cheek. "Naraka always camps within a kilometer or two of friendly villages, so they can feed his men and warn him if police are in the neighborhood. The camp I saw had tents, placed near a river. There are ways to find such things."

"You're right. There are."

Vyasa seemed to see a ray of hope. "You have no further use for me, then?"

"None."

As Bolan spoke, he closed the gap between them with a long stride, whipped his Glock through a sharp roundhouse swing and left Vyasa sprawled on the sofa, unconscious.

"We can take the map," he told Takeri. "It's a good scale. I can match it against those I brought from home."

"What about him?" Takeri asked.

"I'll make a call and have someone take care of him," Bolan said.

Once Bolan finished his call to Brognola to arrange a long-distance pickup, he surveyed the apartment for any trace he might've left behind, then joined Takeri in the outer corridor. They walked back to the service stairwell.

Takeri led the way downstairs, anxious to put the place behind him. Bolan felt vulnerable on their walk back to the rental car, watching for ambushes along the way, but no one tried to intercept them. Only when he had the car in motion once again, cruising Calcutta's crowded streets, did Takeri appear to relax by degrees.

"What now?" he asked, when they had traveled something like a mile.

"We leave tomorrow for the Sundarbans," Bolan replied, "as soon as we can get our act together, make all the arrangements."

"And tonight?" Takeri asked.

"I'm going back to the hotel. If there's someplace you want to go, just tell me how to get there."

"I have an apartment, but—"

"You may have some unwanted visitors waiting to say hello. Where else? A friend's place? Relatives?"

"I don't want to involve them in this trouble."

"You can always bunk with me," Bolan remarked. "The clerk may slap me with an extra charge, but I'm not paying for it, anyway."

"Excuse me?"

"Never mind. I saw some extra bedding in the closet. You can take the chair."

"Thank you."

"No sweat. You'll need your beauty sleep. We're going on safari in the morning, and we won't be back until we bag our limit."

8

It was a quiet night in Bolan's hotel room, with Abhaya Takeri keeping to himself and dozing fitfully while the Executioner savored deep and dreamless sleep, one hand around the Glock beneath his pillow. In the morning, early, they were off to purchase gear they'd need to survive while searching for Naraka's hunters in the Sundarbans.

Bolan already had his weapons, so he concentrated on the clothes and other gear. He bought a set of camouflage fatigues—the tiger-stripe design, in honor of their hunting ground—and army-surplus combat boots designed with mud in mind. His pack and webbing bore a strong resemblance to the gear he'd worn in military service, in another life. One poncho each would serve as rain gear and as bedding. The canteens would make his drinking water smell and taste like plastic, but at least they'd keep it clean. The first-aid kit he bought would handle small emergencies, but antivenin wouldn't travel unrefrigerated, so they had no shield against snakebites.

As for the insects they'd encounter, Bolan flashed back to his Special Forces training and recalled that most jungle natives could smell the pungent chemicals before they saw the person wearing them. Unwilling to take chances, Bolan left the spray behind and counseled his companion to do likewise.

All that remained, at the end of their morning's shopping,

was Takeri's debate over arming himself for the trip. After much muttering and frowning, he agreed to let Bolan procure a weapon for him, whereupon they went back to the pawn-broker on Benjamin Disraeli Street and bought one of the INSAS rifles that Takeri had trained with in the army.

Thus prepared, they drove to Diamond Harbour, where a boat was scheduled to depart for Sonakhali in one hour. They purchased tickets and waited onboard with their gear, getting used to the feel of the boat as it rocked with the swells. The captain waited out his time until departure, but he gained only two other passengers, apparently a married couple on its way home from a visit to the city.

"I guess you don't get seasick?" Bolan asked Takeri, when the boat was under way.

"It doesn't bother me," Takeri said. "The *tigers,* now, they bother me."

"I understand they're fierce, but few and far between," Bolan replied.

"I'll vouch for fierce. As for the rest…" Takeri shrugged. "The state reports three hundred tigers living in the region, but I can't believe they've counted all of them."

"They have those tags now," Bolan said. "Sedate an animal, insert the microchip and you can follow it around for-ever via satellite."

"Perhaps." Takeri sounded skeptical. "But why, then, don't they know where any of the tigers are at any given time?"

Bolan had no reply to that. Instead of answering, he said, "The locals suffer losses every year, I understand."

"It's more like every week, though some of those attacked still manage to survive. You see them in the villages, missing an arm or leg, maybe with half a face. Seeing them makes you wonder if the tiger took the best part."

"They're alive," Bolan replied.

"Of course. And living in a constant state of fear."

"It can't be that bad," Bolan said. "One cat for every five or six hundred square miles? The people must be getting used to them by now."

"They're used to being mauled and eaten," Takeri said.

"And yet, the government does nothing?" Bolan asked.

"You must understand, the tigers are protected. Having passed that law, the state takes it seriously. Their most recent effort to prevent tiger attacks involved a group of mannequins or dummies, fitted with electric wires and batteries. A tiger sees the dummy, thinks it is a man and springs—only to get a numbing shock. In theory, the cats thus chastised would avoid future contact with villagers."

"Adverse conditioning."

"Correct."

"Except?"

"Except," Takeri said, "the dummies do not walk, run, speak, or smell like human beings. To my knowledge, there are no reports of tigers mauling mannequins, but the attacks on villagers continue."

"So, we'll need to watch our backs," Bolan observed.

"Speaking of that," Takeri said, "there is another brilliant theory that a tiger won't attack a man who's facing it. Supposedly, they always strike their victims from behind, to seize and break the neck. For several years, villagers in the Sundarbans were making masks to wear behind their heads, becoming two-faced as it were, to fool the tigers sneaking up behind them."

"Did it work?" Bolan asked.

"No. Over the past four years, at least a dozen tiger victims have been found with masks nearby. The cats don't care."

"We'll stay alert, then. Sleep in shifts. I didn't come halfway around the world to be cat food."

"It isn't only tigers where we're going," Takeri said. "There are crocodiles, cobras and kraits, stingrays and sharks in the waterways that reach the sea. Mosquitoes, spiders, ants and scorpions. All that, without the bandits. There's a reason why police escort all parties entering the Sundarbans."

"About that escort," Bolan asked Takeri. "How do we avoid it?"

"Caution, and a bit of bribery," his guide explained. "You'll likely have to buy a boat, instead of renting one, since owners won't expect a two-man party to return alive."

"And what do you expect?"

"It will be difficult. We have a chance, but honestly—" Takeri stopped and shook his head. "I just don't know."

"Feel better with the rifle, though?"

"Not yet. Perhaps when it is loaded. I'm no great hunter, though."

"This isn't a safari."

"But we're hunting all the same."

Leaning against the rail, watching the wooded coastline pass a few yards from the boat, Bolan considered that. Takeri might turn out to be a liability if Bolan had misjudged him, but he couldn't head into the Sundarbans without a comrade to interpret if he had to speak with native villagers. Alone, his chances of locating Naraka's camp were something close to zero.

"Were you trained in country similar to this?" Bolan asked.

"Yes. Not in the Sundarbans, per se, but farther east."

"It all comes back to you."

"That's my concern," Takeri said. "It's coming back to me already. Hot and cold. Wet all the time. Snakes and insects everywhere."

"You're not a fan of camping, then?"

"I've always hated it," Takeri said. "Perhaps, if we had tents—"

"Too much to carry," Bolan said. "You'll thank me later, when your back's not breaking from the extra weight."

"I doubt that very much," Takeri answered with a crooked smile.

"Okay, then," Bolan said. "Forget about the snakes and tigers. Tell me more about Naraka, if you can."

Where to begin? Takeri thought.

"You've read his dossier?" he asked.

"One version of it, anyway," Bolan replied. "I'm less concerned with facts and figures, now, than what's inside his heart and head."

Takeri frowned. "I can't swear that he has a heart, although some of the people love him. He's a hero to them, just for killing tigers. It's a bit ridiculous, but makes sense from their perspective. Cats kill villagers. Naraka kills the cats."

"The enemy of my enemy is my friend," Bolan said.

"Correct. And he pays them, of course, for supplies and assistance with various tasks. Most of the people in the Sundarbans are fishermen, hunters or honey-gatherers. Naraka likely pays them more for one small job than some earn in a year. He can afford it, with the thefts and the black-market traffic."

"That's why locals like him," Bolan said. "I need more insight on the man himself."

Takeri thought about the documents he'd studied, most of them supplied by Captain Gupta in frustration that his hands were tied.

"He was once a city boy," Takeri said. "Born in Calcutta, where his parents either died or left Naraka to fend for himself on the streets. Such things happen here, I'm afraid."

"They happen everywhere."

"Perhaps. In any case, Naraka managed to survive by wit and wile, a thief and brawler, drawn at some point in his youth to poaching. Probably, he met one of the outlaw hunters on a visit to the city and was dazzled by his money. Once he proved himself with some kind of illegal chores, Naraka might be taken on as an apprentice, lifted from Calcutta, taught the fine points of survival in the bush."

"Like boot camp," Bolan said.

"Except that in Naraka's case, he never left the service. Once he was accepted and became a member of the team, perhaps he found that he enjoyed it. Killing. Living in the wild. No doubt it has a measure of appeal, for some."

"But he was caught," Bolan observed.

"Indeed. Caught and convicted, but the prison could not hold him."

"So I've heard."

"It was a bloody business, the escape, but still it helped to build his legend. Killing one guard inside the prison, then escaping with another and—"

"I read the file," the Executioner said.

"But you may not understand the mind-set of these people. They are poor, perhaps beyond your concept of the term. Compared to these, the poorest people in your nation would seem affluent. Some of them have been poachers at one time, or they have broken other laws while trying to survive."

"I've never bought the argument that crime is necessary for survival," Bolan said.

"I daresay that you've never starved, or seen your children starving. Never mind. Where poaching is concerned, we have a conflict of two cultures. Natives of the Sundarbans have fished and hunted there for countless generations. Suddenly, the government informs them that they may no longer kill the tigers, even if the tigers threaten them. The politicians in Calcutta and New Delhi naturally have no fear of tigers. They will never be devoured in their homes, mauled in their cars, or stalked on city streets. Out here…it is a different world."

"Naraka isn't killing to defend himself," Bolan replied. "Not tigers, elephants, or tourists. Even if you try to argue that he kills police and game wardens in self-defense, it won't stand up. His crimes preceded their attempts to cage him."

"We agree on that," Takeri said. "But neither of us live here, in the Sundarbans. If we did, if we were born and raised here in the shadow of the forest, we might hold a different view."

Bolan did not reply to that. Instead, he changed directions. "If we don't stop him, when he finally runs out of elephants and tigers, then what will Naraka do?"

"No one believes he'll live that long," Takeri said. "Or, possibly, some think he is immortal. Who can say? Without the tigers and the ivory, he'd likely deal in drugs or weapons. Such a man, with his background, cannot exist within the law."

"That's something else that we agree on," Bolan said. "But stopping him may not be such a simple thing as you suppose."

"I never said it would be simple," the American replied.

"But still, you came alone."

"Maybe I don't play well with others."

"Ah. How fortunate for me, in that case, to be traveling with you."

"Nobody drafted you," Bolan replied. "Everything we do in life involves choices."

And he was right, of course. Takeri had been making choices since he joined the army, and throughout the years since his discharge. He'd chosen covert operations when the office world of nine-to-five failed to excite him, and he'd had no serious regrets until the tall American had walked into his life. Now, here he was, embarked upon a jungle odyssey that might well end in death for both of them.

"How many soldiers does Naraka have?" Bolan asked.

"I'm not sure," Takeri answered. "I have never heard a number quoted that I can recall. If there were many, like an army, I suppose New Delhi would have branded them as rebels. At a guess, two dozen, more or less."

"All living in the swamp?"

"Naraka and the hard-core hunters, yes. They have friends in Calcutta and elsewhere, of course."

"Like those who tried to take you out last night?"

"Possibly, although Vyasa may have hired them. There is never any felon shortage in Calcutta," Takeri said.

"Assuming that's the case, will they forget about you, now that he's in no position to pay off on the contract?" Bolan asked.

Takeri had thought of that problem himself. Vyasa's removal might call off the hunters, or they might continue until they got tired of the game. "I focus on one problem at a time," Takeri said. "Right now, I have Naraka and the Sundarbans to think of. If we find him and survive to tell the tale, then I'll think about who wants to kill me in Calcutta."

"Fair enough," Bolan replied. "One battle at a time."

The tall man seemed at ease, as they continued on their way, but Takeri freely admitted to himself that he couldn't read the American's feelings.

The man was fit, well trained, and capable of wreaking havoc on his enemies. He had a calculating mind, and he was cold when the subject was killing.

Not the prescription for a lifelong friend, perhaps. But at the moment, as they sailed into the dark heart of the Sundarbans, Takeri hoped the American was the man to bring him out alive.

9

Balahadra Naraka hated receiving bad news. He'd heard enough of it to last a lifetime—two or three lifetimes, in fact—and enough was enough. He'd reached an age where only good news was welcome, and messengers sometimes suffered accordingly.

Reclining in his camp chair, at the threshold of his tent, Naraka heard the runner coming before the young man was visible. News always roused the camp, particularly when it issued from Calcutta. Even though his men had no idea what Naraka was doing or thinking, they all longed to be a part of the scheme, craving some cast-off crumb of information from his table.

Today, perhaps, he would treat them—but only if the news was good.

The runner was young, and new to the camp, the cousin of a person Naraka had learned to trust over long years of hunting and hiding together. Blood counted in the Sundarbans, although it wouldn't save the young man if he failed Naraka in a way that merited elimination. Every member of his company was well acquainted with Naraka's rules. They understood and they obeyed—or else.

Jalil Salmalin joined Naraka, crouching by his chair to say, unnecessarily, "Asura has returned."

"I have two eyes," Naraka answered, not unkindly, as a

matter of instruction. He sat waiting, patiently, an INSAS rifle with a folding buttstock braced across his knees, as one of the camp's sentries escorted the runner to his tent.

Asura had a winded look and had to have run the last few miles. The effort did him credit, though it might not save him if his news displeased Naraka.

A dozen hunters trailed Asura and his escort as they neared Naraka's tent. A glare from their commander stopped them cold, even before Salmalin shouted at them to go about their business and permit Naraka to receive his latest bulletin in peace. The others wandered off, some of them muttering, but none defied the order—or the glare.

At last the young man stood before him, and Naraka said, "Asura. You've returned with tidings from the city, yes?"

Asura ducked his head, a cautionary bow, and said, "I have."

"Then, by all means, share your news."

The runner hesitated, clutching his hands in front of him, almost as if in prayer. "It is…unfortunate," he said.

Breathing slowly, trying not to grind his teeth behind his thick mustache, Naraka answered, "Nonetheless, tell us."

"Girish Vyasa has disappeared. There were signs of struggle in his apartment, the police say. They are looking for a youth, believed to be his lover. Neighbors say they argued on the night he went missing."

Naraka read the messenger's expression. "You do not believe this story?"

"It may well be true, but…"

"Speak freely."

"There were strangers in Vyasa's building that night. An inspector who apparently does not exist among the city's workers, and another man who may have been a European or Australian."

"May have been?"

Asura shrugged. "He was a white man, tall. That's all the

doorman knew. He never heard the white man speak, and he asked for no credentials."

"Very well." The tension in Naraka's body made his muscles clench. He stared into Asura's eyes and said, "You have more news."

"Yes, sir. I think the false inspector was the man you sent me to inquire about. The one who has been asking questions in Calcutta about ivory and tiger pelts. About Vyasa's business."

"That one." Naraka turned to Salmalin. "What was his name?"

"Takeri," Salmalin replied.

"Of course." Facing Asura once again, Naraka asked, "What makes you think so?"

"An attempt was made to silence him last night, before Vyasa was attacked. The nosy one escaped, assisted by a white man with a pistol."

"Ah." Naraka bit his tongue, tasting a hint of salty blood. "Can anyone describe this man?"

"A white man, as I said. He has dark hair, a complexion darker than you might expect from Europe. He fights well and travels armed."

"Not much to work on," Naraka said tersely. He was pleased to see Asura cringe before he added, "But it may just be enough. Go on. Refresh yourself. You've traveled far."

Naraka waved the youth away and watched him leave. The news would soon be spread throughout his camp, and that was fine with him, if it encouraged his small troupe to stay alert.

Turning again to Salmalin, Naraka asked, "You understand the meaning of this message, do you not, Jalil?"

"Of course. But…"

Vishnu help us! Naraka thought.

Rising from his chair, Naraka clutched Salmalin's arm in

an unyielding grip. Salmalin grimaced, but he didn't dare retreat or even flinch.

"They're coming for us," Naraka said. "Anyone can see that."

"Who is coming?"

"The white man and his companion from Calcutta, at the very least. Whether they bring more with them, we shall have to wait and see."

"How can you know this?" Salmalin asked, mystified.

"They have exhausted the channels of inquiry in Calcutta. When they took Girish Vyasa, they were telling us the city holds no more in store for them."

"They took Vyasa? But the lover—"

"Forget about him. He didn't take Vyasa."

"The police—"

"Are either foolish or concealing information. Our nameless European got to Vyasa, and he'll come for me."

"How will he find you—I mean *us?*"

"You've met Vyasa, Jalil. Did he strike you as a brave man?"

"Arrogant and greedy," Salmalin replied. "Not brave."

"Well, there you are."

"I still don't see—"

"He will have told the strangers where to find us. Possibly, they are already on their way."

"Vyasa doesn't know where we are camped at any given time," Salmalin said.

"He was a greedy coward, not a fool. They won't have the exact coordinates, but these men are probably resourceful. They will find us if they try."

"Not if I find them first," Salmalin said.

"Do that," Naraka ordered. "It would please me very much."

"It shall be done."

"Oh, and Jalil?"

"Yes, sir?"

"Bring me their heads."

BOLAN AND TAKERI disembarked at Sonakhali, where a small crowd of prospective tour guides stood waiting for them on the dock. Bolan ignored them, following his contact in search of someone who would let them have a boat without the standard complement of pilot, guide and armed escorts. On their fifth try, they found an old man willing to ignore the law if he was paid enough to cover the official hassles and the likely loss of one old motor launch.

Bolan surveyed the boat, climbed in and checked its welds, rocked it from side to side and scrutinized the outboard motor. When it started on the first attempt, he nodded to the owner and produced enough cash to include four five-gallon cans of gasoline.

With transportation thus secured, the men went shopping for food. They bought dried beef and fruit, together with canned items that would keep as long as they were sealed. They wanted nothing that would demand a fire. A pharmacist sold them tablets that would purify the rankest water, make it fit for drinking, even though the taste would be unpleasant.

It was late afternoon before they reached the dock again and loaded their provisions in the launch, but Bolan meant to start out. He ignored Takeri's protests that they ought to wait for morning, make a fresh start with sunrise.

"We've wasted too much time," Bolan told his navigator. "If Naraka knows about Vyasa and the rest of it, he may be moving camp again already. I don't want to chase him any longer than we have to."

"Very well. But in the dark—"

"We likely wouldn't find his camp our first night out, regardless," Bolan interjected. "We can camp or sleep in the launch."

Takeri clearly wasn't happy with the prospect of sleeping on the ground in tiger country, but he raised no more objections. He helped Bolan cast off the lines, then took his maps forward and waited while Bolan fired up the outboard and the boat moved away from the dock.

They followed the coastline for an hour, while the sun lowered slowly and the river traffic thinned around them. No officially sanctioned excursions would leave Sonakhali so late in the day, but their departure had apparently gone unobserved by the authorities. When they were out of sight and earshot from the docks, Bolan inquired, "Is someone likely to come after us?"

Takeri shrugged. "I don't know the procedure, but I doubt it. Where would they begin to look?"

"And if they spot us on the water, while they're taking out another tour?"

"That is another question," Takeri said. "They might stop us and insist we come aboard, then take the launch in tow. We should avoid them if we can."

"Sounds like a plan."

Bolan had no intention of colliding with police or game wardens if he could help it, but he didn't know which routes they used for normal tours, or if those routes were changed from time to time. He and Takeri would be forced to stay alert, not only for their prey and any villagers who might know where Naraka could be found, but also for the tourist boats and regular patrols.

Naraka, he supposed, wouldn't pitch camp beside a waterway used frequently by troops. The trick was finding out which rivers bore the brunt of traffic and avoiding them, while picking out a likely place for poachers to bed down.

At least they weren't on foot yet, slogging through the jungle in a sweaty daze while leeches wriggled underneath their clothes and feasted on their blood, surrounded by a swarm of biting flies. The mosquitoes found them soon enough, but the tiny vampires were merely a passing inconvenience.

The Executioner was thinking about larger predators, stalk-

ing on two legs and on four. Either could kill a man within
the time required to realize that he had made one last, fatal
mistake. The trick was to avoid those errors, see the hunters
coming, and respond with enough force to stop them in their
tracks before they made a kill.

For all of his experience in jungles, the Sundarbans were
alien to Bolan. He was used to hiking, hacking vines and
ferns to clear a path or slinking through them like a shadow,
searching out his enemies. Travel by launch, while far less tax-
ing on the muscles, took its toll on Bolan's nerves.

They were exposed on the water, to anyone and anything
ashore. No matter how they watched the forest gliding past,
Bolan had no hope of detecting watchers who were wise
enough to hang back in the shadows, under cover, and observe
them without coming to the water's edge. The crocodiles had
no such qualms. Some slid into the murky water as they
passed, while others gaped at them from mud banks where
they sunned themselves.

Naraka's men would not be so exposed, at least until they
opened fire from ambush. If it came to that, Bolan knew the
only hope would lie in speed and trusting that the gunmen
would not split their force to fire from both sides of the waterway. If he and Takeri were sucked into a cross fire, if their
enemies had any weapons heavier than rifles, they might have
to swim.

And then, he knew, it would be touch-and-go to see
whether the crocs or snipers got to them first.

"This way, I think," Takeri said, pointing out the entrance
to a tributary overhung with trees. It would be darker there,
and they'd be closer to the bank on either side, but Bolan had
to trust Takeri's navigation for the moment. Later, if it seemed
that they were getting nowhere, he might have to try a different angle of attack, but it was still too early to usurp his guide.

Some guide, Bolan thought. He's never been here, either.

But at least Takeri was familiar with the region generally, and he had done a portion of his military training on similar terrain. He knew the plants and animals, the people, and the language. Takeri's misgivings were natural and understandable, but he would have to overcome them if he meant to leave the Sundarbans alive.

Off to their left, beyond his line of sight, a muffled coughing sound exploded into a great snarling roar. Bolan faced the sound, one hand coming to rest upon his Steyr AUG, but there was nothing to be seen beyond the wall of trees and undergrowth that grew down to the water's edge.

"A tiger," Takeri said, sounding none too pleased about it. "We are in their country now."

"Let's hope he's not too hungry," Bolan replied.

"They're always hungry. Count on it."

"In that case," Bolan answered, "we need him to know that we'd leave a bad taste in his mouth."

"I don't suppose you'd reconsider this?" Takeri asked.

"Not even close," Bolan replied.

He steered against the current, holding them at midstream while their outboard motor bore them on, into the jungle's dark and pulsing heart.

10

After a long and murky afternoon, night itself came almost as a surprise, as if some giant unseen hand had found a light switch and extinguished day. A short time earlier, Takeri had advised that they find somewhere to tie up the launch, and Bolan had chosen a branch of the stream on their left, which removed them from the path and sight of any passing nocturnal traffic.

Not that he expected any on the course they had been following. They hadn't glimpsed another boat or human since Takeri had selected his diversion from the river four long hours earlier. Bolan considered that a hopeful sign, however, since he didn't think they'd find Naraka's outfit lounging on the bank of a well-traveled waterway.

As they relaxed and ate a simple meal from cans, he thought about the job he'd taken on, the vast expanse of mangrove swamp that he might have to search before he found Naraka—if, indeed, he *ever* found the target. Bolan knew that if he didn't catch a break somehow, somewhere, they could play hide-and-seek for years without result. The Seminoles had done exactly that with U.S. soldiers in the Everglades of Florida, and there had been no sympathetic villagers to aid them.

And no man-eating tigers to distract the hunters.

"So, we're one day in," he told Takeri, careful not to raise his voice, "and still no tigers. What's the deal?"

"They're here," Takeri answered. "You heard one today. The problem isn't seeing them, my friend. It is when *they* see *us*. We're food to them, that's all."

"I hope they're smart enough to pick another item from the menu."

"Oh, they're smart, all right," Takeri said. "I pray we don't find out how smart they are."

Bolan was also hoping that the big cats would let them pass without a nibble. He had come to stop a poacher who had turned to kidnapping and murder, not to kill off specimens of an endangered species, but he didn't plan to be a tiger's midnight snack. If threatened in the swamp by man or beast, the Executioner was ready to defend himself and his companion.

That thought brought a question to mind. "Aside from last night's brawl," he asked Takeri, "have you seen much action?"

"Although I have never killed a man, I trained for it. During my military service, there were no combat emergencies. We raided several homes, on one occasion, going after Sikh extremists, but they offered no significant resistance."

"Pretty much the same, I guess, since you've been working for the Company?" Bolan inquired.

"I'm an observer, more than anything. On two occasions I have infiltrated groups believed to have a violent purpose. One was innocent. The evidence I gathered in the other case sent men to prison. They would kill me if they could, no doubt, but I've survived so far."

"Forgive my saying so, but you don't seem cut out for it," Bolan observed.

"Because I am not rugged, like yourself, or suave like secret agents from the movies? No." Takeri's smile picked up a glint of moonlight filtered through the overhanging trees. "I do not fit the mold—yet, here I am."

"But hating it," Bolan said.

"Truth be told, it's not as bad as I expected."

Jungle Justice

"Yet."

"Tomorrow I may change my mind, you're right. But once committed to a project, I proceed while any hope remains."

"That's good to know."

"I've put your mind at ease, then?"

"If I'd really doubted you, you wouldn't be here," Bolan said.

"In that case, I am pleased to pass inspection."

"I didn't mean—"

"Please, Mr. Cooper, you have not offended me. We Indians have long become accustomed to surprising—and occasionally disappointing—Westerners. It should be said, for your sake, that I only serve the CIA when I believe its interests coincide with those of India. That has not always been the case of late."

"I can't fault you for that," Bolan allowed.

"Thank you for that. In fact—"

Bolan's raised hand, his sudden change in attitude, cut off Takeri's words. A sound had reached the warrior's ears—a kind of thrashing, splashing noise that told him something or someone was making hasty progress through the swamp. The source of that disturbance wasn't near enough to be a danger yet, but it was moving closer to the point where they had moored their launch, approaching from a west-northwesterly direction.

"Do you hear it?" Bolan whispered.

His companion nodded, reaching down to lift the INSAS rifle and place it in his lap.

Bolan had no idea what sort of creature was advancing toward them. It could be a deer, wild hog, even a tiger that had given up on stealth. He was prepared to wait it out to see what happened next, until a pair of human voices started calling to each other through the darkness.

They were men, he recognized that much, but as for meaning…

"It is Hindi," Takeri said, leaning close, his own voice barely audible at three feet. "One says, 'Come this way.' The other says, 'She's over here.'"

"She?"

He could see Takeri shrug despite the darkness. "It could be an animal. A deer, perhaps even a tiger. Sometimes poachers hunt at night."

"Or villagers?"

"It's possible."

A light winked in the not-too-distant darkness, there and gone. A flashlight's beam. It wasn't aimed in their direction, but the next time Bolan saw it, it was closer. And the voices chasing it were louder, more excited.

"Come on," Bolan told his guide. "We need to check this out."

TAKERI DIDN'T WANT to leave the launch, but neither did he care to challenge Bolan at the moment, when the tall American was so intent on tracking the disturbers of their privacy. He was intrigued, also, as to the prey these unseen hunters stalked by night, though it would not have been enough to draw him from the launch alone.

The American was first ashore, an agile leap across the boat's gunwale that landed him surefooted on the muddy shore. Takeri tried to emulate him, nearly slipped and fell, but caught himself before embarrassment turned into a catastrophe.

With two men, maybe more, advancing toward the point where they had tied the launch, Takeri knew that noise had to be avoided at all cost. He focused on the voices, on the bobbing, flashing light in front of him, and on the shadow-shape of his companion as he led the way through clinging undergrowth to intercept the trackers.

As they closed the gap, Takeri had less problem making out and translating the others' words. Two voices only, which was good—unless they were the only two of several who were allowed to speak. Takeri had no wish to meet Naraka's band of seasoned hunters in the dark, on ground they knew as well as he knew certain sectors of Calcutta.

Still, if there were only two…

"This way!" one of the unseen men called out.

"I tell you, she is here!" the other voice replied.

They started cursing one another then, giving Takeri time to think about exactly who or what *she* was. Of course, he didn't know the men, which limited his frame of reference. If they were villagers, they might be searching for a girl or woman who was lost.

But if they were Naraka's men…

Takeri clutched the INSAS rifle to his chest, thumb resting near the safety lever, while he prayed the muddy soil beneath his feet would stop its telltale sucking sounds. The American seemed to have a silent way of moving, almost supernatural, as if his feet did not quite touch the ground.

Ridiculous!

He was a man like any other, trained to creep and fight in darkness over unfamiliar ground. Takeri had been trained, as well, but he'd grown rusty over time as his new calling kept him mostly in the city, pounding pavement, living in a different kind of jungle.

Take your time, he thought. Remember and relax.

By slow degrees, Takeri found his rhythm, pleased to note that his steps were nearly silent, that the ferns and dangling vines slid past him without tripping him or snatching at his clothes.

It's no great trick, Takeri told himself. I'm doing it!

And suddenly, he glanced up from the trail to find that his colleague had disappeared.

Takeri froze, afraid to take another step until he worked out where the gruff American had gone. Only his head and eyes moved as he scanned the night, sweeping 180 degrees from left to right and back again, without a hit.

In front of him, the light and calling voices had grown closer, maybe halved the gap, and now Takeri found himself alone. He knew the American had not turned back—but where, then, had he gone?

A faint hiss in his left ear drew Takeri's gaze in that direction. Squinting, hoping for a beam of moonlight to reward him, he eventually saw the subtle movement of an arm raised, waved and lowered.

The Executioner had been crouched no more than fifteen feet in front of Takeri and slightly to his left, a dark blotch in the shadows. If he had not hissed and raised his hand, Takeri might have passed him by, unseen.

Instead, he joined Bolan cautiously, planting his feet precisely on the spongy earth, finding a place to kneel that would not crowd Bolan or leave himself exposed. A massive tree had fallen there. It sheltered them for the moment, and would stop bullets if the rapidly advancing hunters suddenly spotted them.

Slowly, alert to any small metallic noise, Takeri thumbed his rifle's safety toward the firing position. He had a live round in the chamber. He was ready.

Or so he told himself.

The light was closer, sweeping above their heads, flickering off the trees. The men were still advancing, but they spoke less frequently, no longer sounding so convinced that *she* was just in front of them.

As for their prey, Takeri sensed no movement in the space between his shelter and the two advancing hunters. Maybe he had missed it, taken with the light and voices, or perhaps—

The light veered leftward, and a sudden shout exploded from the darkness. "There! I see her!"

Craning forward, following the chase, Takeri glimpsed two man-shapes in the darkness, trudging over mucky ground, crashing through the undergrowth without regard to noise. And was there something else, running ahead of them?

The leading object stumbled, fell. The hunters were upon it in another moment, laughing even though the sprint had left them winded.

"So," one said, "you thought you could outrun us!"

"Not tonight," the other jeered. "Not here!"

A third voice, clearly female, sobbed in answer. "Please, just let me go!"

Bolan was up and moving in a heartbeat, without waiting for Takeri to translate. The mere sound of the woman's voice had been enough to launch him from his place behind the log.

God help us, Takeri thought, as he rose and followed close behind.

"IT WASN'T NICE OF YOU to make us run so far," Darshan Vasitri said.

"Not nice," Ganesh Shakti agreed.

Each held one of the woman's arms. She squirmed between them, trying to escape, but she was held fast, like an insect in a spiderweb. Vasitri watched her, breathing heavily from the exertion of the chase, and found himself excited by her struggles.

"You have led us on a pretty chase," he said.

"A pretty chase," Shakti echoed. An old, annoying habit.

"Why would you do such a thing?" Vasitri asked, twisting her slender arm for emphasis.

"Because you're filthy pigs!" she spit at him.

Her boldness made Vasitri laugh, and Shakti took his cue as always from the older man, cackling as if she'd told the greatest joke on record.

"So, we're pigs, are we? And yet, you sought us out. There must be something that attracts you to the swine, eh?"

Hatred simmered in the lithe young woman's eyes. "You

think I came for you?" she asked him, scornfully. "That makes you a pathetic pig."

Vasitri didn't laugh this time. His rodent eyes had narrowed dangerously. "So, if not for us, then who?" he asked.

"Who else?" she taunted him. "The one who pulls your strings and makes you dance."

"What dance?" Shakti asked, suddenly confused.

"Quiet!" Vasitri snapped at his companion.

To the woman, then, he said, "We're all there is for you. Your journey ends with us—but not, I think, before you share your secrets."

With a lightning move, Vasitri cranked the woman's arm behind her back, hoisting it high between her shoulder blades. The sudden strain put her on tiptoes, spine arched, trying to reduce the pain.

Vasitri passed the flashlight to Shakti with a curt demand. "Take this." His free hand then began to roam the struggling woman's body, tracing lines and contours, while she wriggled and cursed him.

Amused, Vasitri gave her arm another vicious twist. "You don't like being touched? Maybe a broken arm will change your mind."

"A broken arm," Shakti said, chuckling as he tried to twist her other arm one-handed.

Relenting in the face of so much pain, she sobbed, "What do you want?"

"You're not so young and innocent as you pretend to be," Vasitri said. "We'll hear about this man you seek—but not just yet. First, we deserve a fair reward for saving you."

"A fair reward," Shakti repeated, almost drooling.

"If we hadn't come along, a tiger might have eaten you."

Shakti was grinning, doglike. "Eaten you," he said.

"A kiss, I think," Vasitri said. "Or something more."

"More," Shakti urged. "Much more."

"I'll die first," the woman said.

"I don't think so," Vasitri repeated. "After, possibly. But not before."

The young woman wore a man's shirt, and Vasitri fumbled with the buttons briefly, then gave up and ripped it open, from her neck down to her waist, where it tucked into denim pants. Vasitri reached inside, fondling, and had to twist her arm again as she half turned away from him.

"You might as well enjoy it, little one," he said. "We have all night."

"All night," Shakti said, reaching toward her with his hand that held the flashlight, clumsily, its bright beam flaring in Vasitri's eyes.

"Get that damned light out of—"

The gunshot made Vasitri flinch as the light swung away from his face and left him blinking. He saw Shakti fall and recoiled, still clinging to the woman as she tried to wrench away from him. He dropped instinctively into a crouch, dragging the woman with him, hauling her around to place her wriggling form between himself and the apparent origin of the gunshot.

Shakti was still alive, it seemed, but he made ghastly gurgling sounds, as if he were drowning. Without the light, Vasitri didn't bother trying to assess Shakti's condition. He was shot, and he would live or die without Vasitri's fumbling first-aid efforts.

"This way!" he hissed at the woman, beginning to duckwalk backward, still using her as an unwilling shield while he sought decent cover. They reached a mangrove, with its massive spreading roots, and Vasitri pulled his captive after him into its shadow.

"Stay!" he ordered, as if she were a dog, then struck her with a stunning backhand to enforce the point. She slumped, giving Vasitri time to free his rifle from its shoulder sling and search for targets in the night.

In retrospect, it had been foolish of him to pursue the woman, bringing only stupid Shakti for support. But it was mostly her fault, he thought, suddenly appearing out of nowhere in the swamp, enticing him away from camp. Vasitri didn't know if it had been a trap from the beginning, or if they had stumbled onto enemies by chance, despite the woman, but he cursed her for luring him with sex and mystery.

In fact, Vasitri thought, he ought to kill her immediately, before she caused him further trouble.

Rising from his crouch, Vasitri took a short step backward, brought the rifle to his shoulder and prepared to fire. The woman glared at him through angry tears, unyielding, refusing to beg for mercy.

Too bad, Vasitri thought. It was a waste.

His finger tightened on the trigger, but the shot sounded remote, almost an echo, rather than the sharp crack he'd expected. Even as the bullet ripped into his chest, Darshan Vasitri recognized his last mistake and cursed the darkness that enveloped him.

THE FIRST OF TWO MEN shot was still alive when Bolan reached him. The man was fumbling for his gun. Bolan didn't want to give any trackers in the night another chance to fix on his position. Stooping, he drew the K-Bar combat knife from his belt and whipped its blade smoothly across the gurgling throat.

Silence.

Takeri had the woman and was leading her toward Bolan without much resistance on her part. She'd fought the others more aggressively, and since she wasn't wounded, Bolan guessed that watching two men die had taken something out of her.

At least for the moment.

"We'll take her to the launch," Bolan said. "Time enough to talk when we're away from here."

He led the way, Takeri following, the woman between them. Bolan watched the trail while listening to her, prepared to move if she regained her nerve and bolted from the path.

She was a complication that he didn't want, but Bolan felt a need to find out what had brought her to this killing place at night, pursued by ruffians who would've raped her, at the very least. Her clothing struck him as unusual for a village woman, though his knowledge in that regard was strictly limited. Above all else, he had to know what impact she might have upon his mission. Then he could decide what he should do with her.

The launch was moored a quarter mile or so from where he'd shot the two gunmen. It wasn't far, but in the darkness they might still avoid a search party if anyone came looking for the fallen pair. There'd been no calls, no other lights or noises of pursuit so far, and Bolan took that as a hopeful sign. Maybe the two swamp dwellers had been on their own, a pair of misfits in the mode of something from *Deliverance.*

Maybe.

But if the two were local villagers, they would be missed, searched for, eventually found. Likewise, if they worked for Naraka, he was likely to notice their absence sooner, rather than later.

Good news, bad news.

If the two men were Naraka's, it could mean the poacher's camp was somewhere close at hand. They might be scouts dispatched to survey virgin territory, far from their master's lair. In the first case, their deaths would likely launch a full-scale search for enemies. The other angle meant that Bolan and Takeri were no closer to Naraka than they had been when they hired the launch.

The woman balked at the sight of the tiny boat, then boarded when Takeri spoke to her in Hindi. Even then, she wouldn't let Takeri help her, pulled away from his attempt to steady her.

They sat, and Bolan let another moment pass before he spoke, testing the night for any sounds suggesting a pursuit. When he heard nothing but the high-pitched cries of bats wheeling above his head, he faced the woman, studying her face and form as best he could by moonlight.

She was relatively young, and from the flashlight glimpses he'd obtained during the botched assault, Bolan already knew she was attractive. She'd ignored the torn shirt while they marched back to the river, but she held it clutched together now, with her left hand.

"We should find something else for her to wear," Bolan said.

"I have two more shirts," Takeri answered. "They're too large, but they will cover her, at least."

"Okay."

Takeri fetched his pack, rummaged inside it and produced a spare shirt, which he handed to the woman. She accepted it without comment and put it on over the ruined shirt she wore, leaving the tails outside her denim jeans.

She said something in Hindi, and Takeri smiled. "It's very strange, she says," he translated.

"What is?" Bolan asked.

And the woman answered for herself in perfect English. "It's the first time men have kidnapped me to give me clothes."

11

Bolan recovered from his surprise in time to say, "We're not kidnapping you. In fact, unless I'm very much mistaken, we just saved your life."

"That doesn't give you any right to hold me," the woman replied.

"You're right," he said. "Go."

She blinked at him, her turn to be surprised. "What do you mean?" she asked.

"You're free to go. Good luck."

"But I...those men..."

"They're dead," Bolan assured her. "Unless you're afraid of ghosts, they shouldn't be a problem."

"What if there are others?"

"I don't hear anything," Bolan said. "If you start now, you ought to have a good head start by dawn. Chances are, they won't pick up your trail."

Moonlight flashed on a teary glint in her right eye, but Bolan couldn't tell if she was acting, or sincerely worried. "I've lost all my gear," she told him. "And my weapon. How will I survive?"

"You got here somehow," Bolan said. "We don't have much to spare, but we can let you have a little food. Walk back the way we came a quarter mile, and you'll find rifles, bandoliers of ammunition, everything you need."

"Damn it!" she flared, "what do you want from me?"

Bolan decided it was time to push his luck. "Nothing," he answered. "We're just passing through and stopped to help you out. Now, if you'll run along, we'd like to get some sleep."

"You aren't just visiting the Sundarbans," she said, eyeing the assault rifles in Bolan's lap.

"And you are, I suppose?"

"Perhaps."

"Sorry. We don't need any bedtime fairy tales. Bye-bye."

"You're hunting," she suggested, "but your weapons aren't for deer or tigers. Hunting men, I think. But if it was officially approved, you'd both be wearing uniforms."

"Assuming that you're right," Bolan replied, "that makes us killers. What's to stop us from getting rid of you right now?"

"You would have done that earlier, or let the others do it for you. I believe you are not evil men, but you have come to find one. Possibly to slay him."

"Oh?"

She shrugged. "Two men would never come alone if they intended to arrest the man I'm thinking of. With the support he has, it is impossible. But two might find a way to kill him if they could get close enough."

"You must've hit your head back there," Bolan said. "You're hallucinating."

"I can help you," she insisted, "if you seek the same man I do."

Bolan took another chance. "And who would that be?"

"Balahadra Naraka. I will not rest until I've seen him dead."

"You're out here on a mission, then?" Bolan asked.

"Yes. A mission of revenge."

"You'd better fill us in," he said. "Beginning with your name."

"Indra Mehadi," she replied. "May I know yours?"

"Matt Cooper."

She half turned toward Takeri, waiting, and the flustered

guide gave her his real name. In the darkness, Bolan couldn't tell if he was blushing.

"So," she said, "we know one another now."

"Not even close," Bolan said. "Why are you after Naraka?"

"It's a story simply told," Mehadi replied. "My father was a game warden here on the Sundarbans preserve. He loved the tigers most of all, and hated those who killed them for their skins. Naraka murdered him. His head was…never found."

"I'm sorry," Bolan said. "How long ago was this?"

"Eleven months."

"You waited all that time to hunt him down?"

"My mother needed me. After my father's death, her mind…she never was the same. Sad always, never smiling, barely stepping out of doors. She needed care."

"And now?"

"She died last month. A suicide, the doctors say, but it's Naraka's fault. I needed time to learn about him, find out where he hides. I would have found him, too, if not for those two pigs you shot."

"Those two, or someone else," Bolan replied. "Maybe a tiger sees you coming, and he hasn't eaten for a while."

"I'm not afraid of tigers," she assured him.

"What about trained killers? Everyone keeps telling me Naraka's killed a hundred men or more, most of them trained with firearms and in self-defense. What makes you good enough to sneak in past his men and take him out?"

"I have advantages," she said.

"Such as?"

"I am a woman. Some find me attractive."

"Like the two we met tonight," Bolan said.

"That was just bad luck."

"Exactly," Bolan replied. "If we hadn't come by, they would've killed you when they started getting tired."

"Or shown me to Naraka, possibly," she said.

"Would that be an improvement?"

"If it put me close enough to kill him, even with my dying breath, then yes!"

"So, that's your plan?" he asked. "Wander around the swamp, hoping to find a rapist who will pass you to Naraka when he's finished with you?"

"I'm not a fool!" she snapped. "I told you that I brought a weapon and equipment, but—"

"You lost it," Bolan finished for her.

"You make sport of me," she said.

"Not even close. I'm wondering what we should do with you."

"I'll help you. Since we both want the same thing—"

"I haven't said that," Bolan said.

"Nor have you denied it. If I am mistaken, if you are not looking for Naraka to destroy him, then by all means let me have the food you offered earlier, and I'll be on my way."

It was a bluff, but Bolan didn't feel like calling it. What was the point? Now that he'd met this woman and heard her story, Bolan had no reason to suppose she'd leave the hunt to him. Most likely, she'd continue blundering around the game preserve until Naraka's hunters captured her a second time—and then, when they began to work on her, she might attempt to save herself by spilling what she knew about his mission.

On the other hand, perhaps she'd greet her death in silence, fortified by hatred of their common enemy.

That prospect failed to offer any consolation. Having saved her life—or, at the very least, her honor—from the pair of would-be rapists, Bolan felt responsible to some extent for what befell the woman next. He didn't buy the Asian princi-ple that one who saved a life was bound to nurture and pro-tect it ever afterward, but in the present situation, Bolan knew

it would be tantamount to murder if he sent the young woman
into the swamplands on her own.

"All right," he said reluctantly. "Impress me. Tell me what
you know."

12

Balahadra Naraka was pleased with the day's work. His men had tracked and killed another tiger, this one a mature male, and they were busy taking it apart for transport to the market. He could hear them laughing as they worked by firelight, making sure that all was ready for the morning boat.

Tigers were marvelous creatures. No part of them was wasted, and each bit put money in Naraka's pocket. He knew a prime pelt, like the one under preparation in his camp, might sell to some fat armchair "sportsman" for five or six thousand U.S. dollars, but that was only the beginning for a wily poacher. Asian pharmacists and sorcerers vied daily for the tiger relics that Naraka could supply, their competition driving prices ever higher.

Naraka sipped a cup of wine while taking mental inventory of the cat they'd killed that afternoon. Its teeth and claws were often worn as lucky charms, but both were also valued as medicinal remedies—powdered teeth to cure fevers, the ground-up claws as sedatives to treat insomnia. Tiger eyes, priced at almost two hundred dollars per pair, were used to treat malaria and epilepsy. The cat's brain was supposed to be a remedy for laziness and acne. Its nose leather was applied by countless devotees to patch superficial wounds. A tiger's whiskers were supposed to cure toothache.

Moving along the body, tiger fat was said to be a curative

for leprosy and rheumatism. Bile from the liver and the gall bladder allegedly relieved convulsions in children suffering from spinal meningitis. The tiger's penis was a classic aphrodisiac, distilled into potions or boiled into soup at an average price tag of three hundred U.S. dollars per bowl. The tail was used to treat assorted skin diseases. Even tiger dung was precious, used by various practitioners to treat boils, hemorrhoids and alcoholism.

Naraka grimaced at the thought and took another sip of wine.

Surprisingly, the most expensive portion of a tiger was its skeleton. The bones, allegedly, possessed magical curative powers, employed in various forms as an anti-inflammatory drug for rheumatism and arthritis, to relieve general weakness, cure headaches, stop dysentery, and to relieve stiffness or paralysis of the legs and lower back. Wholesale prices for tiger bone ranged from $860 to $1,280 per kilogram, but prices were higher for leg bones, associated in the Asian mind with predatory power. A tiger's humerus might sell for $1,500 by itself, in Seoul or Tokyo.

Once purchased on the wholesale market, tiger bones were marketed in two ways. Traditional pharmacies and physicians stocked whole bones intact, shaving off tiny slivers for individual patients as prescribed. More modern remedies incorporated bone meal into pills, powders and wine—mostly produced in China and South Korea, for export through Hong Kong to markets worldwide. In Asian communities around the world, an estimated twenty-nine million people relied on traditional folk remedies to correct or preserve their health.

And every one of them was a potential customer for Balahadra Naraka.

Black-market ivory, by contrast, sold for an average seventeen U.S. dollars per pound, although deflation hadn't kept Naraka and his men from killing elephants. Where there was money to be made, in small or large amounts, Naraka was prepared to strike. It also pleased him to harass the game wardens who'd once sent him to prison on a poaching charge—to rub their noses in the stench of failure, torment them and kill them when he had the chance.

Predictably, Naraka did not view his long crusade against authority as being pathological. In his mind, he had always been the victim, through the years of childhood poverty that made him steal to the persecution by police when he was caught. The slaughter of endangered species, to Naraka, was a doubly sweet pastime: it made him wealthy, even as it showcased his supreme defiance for the soft men in their suits and fancy houses, paid to dictate how and where the lower classes ought to live.

In his reflective moments, Naraka saw himself as a rebel. He was struggling against oppressors who had held his people down for centuries. If asked precisely who his people were, he might have pointed to the other men in camp or named the poor villagers of the Sundarbans, though he had no roots there. But Naraka seldom contemplated that part of his rebel fantasy, because he had no great interest in anyone except himself.

Then again, he considered, most great men felt the same.

What president, prime minister or king, Naraka might have asked, truly cared more about his nation than his own wealth and well-being. Wars were fought for power, influence and economic spoils. The gibberish about "liberty" and "justice" was a smoke screen, used by fat-cat politicians and their sponsors to disguise their latest power-grab.

It was appropriate, therefore, that when Naraka raged against the system, he struck his adversaries in the pocketbook. He had grown rich at their expense.

The best revenge was living well.

Of course, he knew some critics might suggest that living well did not include a camp site in a mangrove swamp, but everything was relative. Naraka cherished freedom and the reputation he had cultivated over time. He did not crave plush furnishings, silk underwear, gold-plated plumbing and the like. There was a certain charm to living as a fugitive, and he enjoyed it thoroughly.

One final sip of wine, and then—

The shouting ruined it, one of his men running across the compound, calling out his name. Naraka sighed. There was no end to his responsibilities.

"We have found them," the runner gasped.

"Calm yourself, Kotari. Who is found?"

"Darshan Vasitri and Ganesh Shakti. Both dead by gunshots."

Naraka rose at once from his camp chair. "Show me," he said.

"WE'LL HAVE TO LEAVE the launch soon," Takeri said. He was seated in the bow, as usual, examining his maps.

"Just tell me where and when," Bolan replied.

Indra Mehadi sat between them, early-morning sunshine painting blue-black highlights in her hair. She wore it shorter than most women Bolan had seen since landing in Calcutta, trimmed to shoulder length. Despite her recent ordeal, and the fact that she had neither comb nor brush, it framed her oval face attractively. No makeup there, after her long trek through the mangrove swamp, but she required none in the morning light.

Sometime during the night, Mehadi had ditched her ruined shirt and wore only Takeri's, tucked in so that it didn't drape her body like an artist's smock. Her jeans were snug and faded, fraying at the knees. When she stood, Bolan could see the outline of a clasp knife in her right hip pocket. Her hiking shoes were old, but still in decent shape.

"Another mile, perhaps a little more," Takeri said. "We'll have to go on foot from there."

Which meant hiding the launch as best they could to keep Naraka's men or anybody else from finding, stealing or sink-ing it while they were trekking through the jungle. It would be a long walk back to Sonakhali if they lost the boat—assuming they were still in any shape to try it.

The launch was relatively small, no more than twenty feet in length, which helped in terms of its concealability. Bolan still wasn't sure how many men Naraka had, or how they were deployed. Patrolling riverbanks throughout the Sundarbans in search of boats would keep a fair-sized army occupied around the clock, and if Takeri's estimate was accurate, Naraka might have no more than two dozen men on hand. In which case, he supposed, they had a decent chance.

The Executioner wasn't taking anything for granted, recognizing that the odds against them had increased when Mehadi joined the team. While she might be committed to Naraka's downfall, she had already been captured once and lost her gear to enemies. Bolan had no faith in her ability to contribute to the task at hand, and worried that she would endanger them, either by some impulsive action or simply by virtue of demanding care.

As if reading his mind, the woman chose that moment to remark, "I'm not as useless as you may suppose."

"I guess we'll see," Bolan replied.

"I'll prove it to you. Have you located Naraka's base camp?" she asked.

Bolan saw no point in lying to her at the moment. "We're still looking for it," he responded. "Have you got a fix?"

"If you mean the precise location, I do not," she said. "But I'm told there is a village where his men are always welcome, not so far from here."

"Is that where you were going when they found you?" Bolan asked.

"Yes. It was a foolish risk for me to go alone, perhaps."

"Perhaps," Bolan agreed.

"I see that, now. But who would I invite to join my quest

for vengeance, when I have no family remaining in the world?"

"If you know where Naraka's hiding, you could pass that information on to the authorities," Bolan said.

"And for what?" she asked him almost scornfully. "They haven't managed to locate him in the past ten years. No bandit is that lucky. Someone in authority has shielded him."

Bolan could only shrug at that. "You may be right."

"You know I am. Why else are you now hunting him like this, without police or soldiers to assist you?"

"Sometimes less is more," Bolan replied.

"I do not understand."

"Too many bodies, too much racket and confusion," Bolan said. "Lone hunters always see more game than members of a big safari."

"Only if they know where game is to be found," Mehadi stated, smiling as she challenged him.

"Okay, I'll bite," Bolan said. "Where's this village?"

"You are heading in the right direction," she informed him. "If we leave the boat as planned, within another mile, I can direct you overland."

"Meaning you want to come along?" Bolan asked.

"Certainly. I won't be left behind."

"That may not be your choice."

"What, then? Do you intend to leave me with the boat, tied up and helpless? Better you had let me go last night, alone."

"I tried," Bolan reminded her.

"No, no. You only wished to frighten me. I know a fair man when I meet one."

"Don't take anything for granted," Bolan said. "You haven't known me half a day."

"Still, I can tell. You fight for justice."

"Wrong. I'm here to do a job."

"It's all the same," she said with irritating confidence.

"You need to understand something," Bolan replied, raising his voice so that it carried to Takeri's ears, as well. "We don't have time to babysit or hold your hand. If you're directing us somewhere, it means you have to lead, not lag behind. No one's going to carry you. First time you fall behind, we'll leave you flat. And if you cause another incident that's detrimental to our job, you're on your own."

She searched his eyes for any hint of weakness, found none and responded with a nod. "Agreed."

"All right," Bolan said. "Where's this village, then?"

"It has no name, as far as I can tell," Mehadi said. "It lies west of here, perhaps a half-day's march. I have coordinates to find it on a map."

"Let's have those, then," Bolan replied.

"Not yet."

"Why not?" he asked.

"Because you might decide to leave me with the boat if I reveal too much, too soon."

"You mean to go the distance, then."

"I do."

"And what about the finish?" Bolan asked. "You can't pitch in and pull your weight with nothing but a pocketknife."

"I'll manage."

"Will you? When's the last time that you killed a man?"

She had no answer to that question, couldn't even turn the words around on him, since she'd seen him kill two men already. Or maybe he had only killed one of the men who meant to rape her, while Takeri shot the other. Either way, she knew she was the novice of the team, unskilled and virtually unarmed.

"I'll find a weapon when I need it," she assured him. "You don't need to worry about me."

"That's just the point," the Executioner said, nodding toward his partner. "Both of us are forced to think about you every minute, now. You're a distraction at the very least. Maybe a fatal obstacle."

"I'm your best hope of getting to Naraka's camp before he moves again," she replied. "Trust me."

Bolan considered it, then answered, "To a point."

"This is the place," Takeri called out.

Bolan throttled back the motor, slowed the launch and steered it closer to the western shore. "We're looking for a place to stash this tub," he said to Mehadi. "Help Takeri look, will you?"

She went forward, smiling as Takeri turned to glance at her. He was clearly attracted to her. Mehadi recognized the signs, even on short acquaintance, but the previous night's experience with strangers made her reticent to play that card. She didn't think these men would harm her voluntarily, but they were focused on their mission—which, as luck would have it, seemed to be the same as hers. She could not risk dividing them or making them her enemies, when they now represented her best hope of reaching Balahadra Naraka.

"I'm supposed to help you search," she told Takeri.

"So I heard."

"We're looking for a place to hide the boat?"

"As well as possible," he said. "It won't be perfect, but we don't want every fisherman within ten miles to see it by tomorrow."

"Someplace dark and narrow, then," she speculated. "Something tight and uninviting to the casual observer."

"Absolutely."

She frowned, pointing. "What's that? Ahead there, on the left?"

"That shadow?" he inquired.

"There's more," she said. "I'm almost sure of it."

Takeri shuffled farther forward, going to all fours and leaning out to scan the riverbank ahead of them. After a moment, he turned back toward Bolan at the helm, waving a hand and calling out, "Slow here, and to the left. We've found something."

Mehadi felt like correcting him, saying, "*I've* found something," but she kept silent. Anything that helped her rescuers, for now, helped her as well.

Takeri gave directions while Bolan steered the launch, turning it across the river's current and nosing it slowly into a gap in the riverside foliage. Mangrove boughs and hanging vines almost concealed a cutout in the bank with room enough to take the launch with a foot to spare on either side, and with ample water underneath to keep it floating.

It was tight, with branches scraping hungrily over the deck and cabin. Mehadi watched carefully for snakes and spiders in the foliage, but they made it without. By the time their boat's prow bumped against the muddy shore, their stern was hidden by the same green curtain that had masked the inlet from their view.

But not from mine, she thought.

It was an omen. She had proved herself, after the previous night's embarrassing fiasco, and while she knew it wouldn't be enough to win their total confidence, at least she had taken a step in the proper direction.

Bolan killed the motor and they sat in silence for a moment, waiting for the nearby birds and insects to resume their constant background noise. When no one sprang from hiding to surprise them, the men started making ready for the march, checking their packs and weapons, slipping into gear that matched their camouflaged fatigues.

Mehadi, meanwhile, had lost her kit when she was captured. She would be traveling extremely light, with nothing but the clothing on her body—some of it Takeri's—and the folding knife she carried in her pocket. Not much for a journey through the Sundarbans, she thought, but if she came within arm's reach of her intended prey, the knife would serve her well.

And what, then?

She'd thought little, if at all, beyond the moment when she would confront Naraka, tell him who she was and end his worthless life. A part of Mehadi's mind assumed she would be killed in the effort, either cut down on the spot or captured and tormented over days, until her strength ran out. Remembering her parents, she'd been willing to accept that possibility without regrets.

But, the past night she had been introduced to fear. It nibbled at the edge of her resolve, tarnished the stainless steel of her resolve.

Indra Mehadi didn't want to die.

As they prepared to leave the hidden launch, she turned her mind to schemes that might allow her to survive.

TAKERI HELPED THE WOMAN step down from the launch onto the spongy riverbank. One of his hands brushed accidentally against her breast in the process, and he instantly apologized, feeling the startled color in his cheeks.

"It's nothing," she replied.

Nothing. And yet…

He had to focus on the mission that had brought him to the Sundarbans, remembering his personal reluctance to participate. Nothing had changed about the task, except for the young woman's presence as an ill-equipped and unexpected member of the team. Takeri knew he should be angry or distressed at being saddled with a woman on the eve of battle, but he had difficulty acting gruff with her.

Under other circumstances, Takeri thought, he might ask her out to dinner, possibly to see a film. And if she liked him well enough, they might—

"This way," Bolan said, cutting through Takeri's reverie.

Takeri cursed himself. There were no other circumstances, no soft lighting for romance. She was here to kill a man, just as they were. The fact that both their targets were the same bespoke coincidence. It wasn't any sign that they were meant to meet and mingle, that their life paths would be parallel from this point onward.

It was nothing but a cheat.

The most attractive woman he had met in years was nothing but a would-be murderer, embarked upon a suicidal vengeance odyssey.

Mehadi directed them, and Bolan used his compass to confirm the heading she had chosen. Satisfied, he led the way, with her close behind him and Takeri bringing up the rear.

Takeri didn't mind the view. The womanly buttocks rolling in the tight blue jeans, good legs, the curve of her waist—but he was also busy watching out for reptiles that could kill a person in minutes, listening for sounds of human passage through the forest. Waiting for the flash of orange and white that would alert him—probably too late—that they had crossed a tiger's path.

Takeri didn't want to die with two-inch fangs cracking his vertebrae, shearing through his carotid arteries. He didn't want to die at all, in fact, but being eaten while he impotently screamed and wept seemed worst of all. Better to take a bullet in the chest, or feel a cobra's venom coursing through his veins as he began to suffocate.

Worse yet, if he was eaten now, Indra Mehadi would be on hand to watch it. She would hear him shriek in terror, see him shaken like a rag doll, as the tiger had its way with him. It seemed bizarre for him to be embarrassed by the thought of sudden death, but there it was. A new emotion that Takeri hadn't felt before.

Damn women, anyway.

The INSAS rifle in his hands would stop a tiger. He was sure of that. The trick, Takeri realized, was being quick enough and shooting straight enough before the great cat sprang upon him, rode him to the ground, mauled him with razor claws and found its death grip on his neck.

As for the snakes—cobras and kraits, the deadly *tic polonga*—he could only watch each root and vine, each fallen branch, and hope that the others scared them off the trail ahead, instead of irritating them, making them strike at anyone behind.

Takeri barely thought about the wild boars that could rush squealing from the undergrowth and slash him with their tusks, rip through his hamstrings, leaving him lame and bleeding on the trail. And he ignored completely any thought of lurking crocodiles that sometimes wandered far from water, but were more likely to strike Takeri in or near a stream.

There was too much to think about, too many dangers in the swamp. And of them all, the worst was none other than Balahadra Naraka—the very man they'd come to find.

Naraka had killed more men in his time than any tiger in the Sundarbans. The lowest tabulation of his body count averaged ten murders every year, and that was probably conservative. How many others were officially unknown, concealed by circumstance and the environment where Naraka chose to hide? Takeri guessed no one would ever know the answer, but he didn't want to join the grim list of statistics.

Staying alive would be his first priority. Beyond that, helping to eliminate Naraka could be lucrative. But, if compelled to make a choice between his own safety and Mehadi's or Cooper's, would he rise to the occasion? Would he be a hero? he wondered.

Sacrifice had rarely crossed Takeri's mind as an adult, except perhaps in military training, when he was a green recruit. Such things were drilled into a soldier's head in boot camp, but without a war to fight they lacked real context. Advancing toward a real-life enemy, across terrain where life was touch-and-go, Takeri felt a sudden need to take stock of himself.

Was he prepared to risk his life for the American? Or for the woman he barely knew? Would he freeze up in combat? Maybe lose his life because he was afraid to risk it?

Cooper had dispatched both of Mehadi's attackers, taking down the giggler first, then circling through the darkness to surprise the other one. He'd cut the wounded poacher's throat without a moment's hesitation, silencing his raspy voice forever. Through it all, Takeri hadn't frozen—but he hadn't seen a clear shot, either. Hadn't fired his weapon, leaving the other man to perform the dirty work.

He had not proved himself.

Not yet.

But he supposed the time was coming, and he prayed it would not find him wanting. Not in Cooper's eyes, in Mehadi's, or his own.

A day of judgment was approaching, and Takeri hoped that he would pass the test.

13

Naraka stood over the corpses of his men, examining their wounds with a detachment born of long experience with violent death. Both had been shot, that much was plain. A single bullet each, and it appeared that Ganesh Shakti's throat might have been cut, but it was difficult to say.

The swampland's scavengers had been at work before the two dead men were found. Vultures and rats had claimed their share of carrion, followed by ants, worms, beetles, flies. Within another day, at most, the bodies would've been unrecognizable, but they'd been found in time for confirmation that they were—had been—Naraka's men.

They hadn't been the best, of course.

On any scale of ranking, Shakti would be near the bottom, leader of village idiots, but loyal in his way. Vasitri had been somewhat better, but the pair of them together still barely possessed a single working brain. Both were impulsive, prone to drunkenness, likely to make small tasks more difficult than necessary.

Together, they were dead.

On their last day alive, Vasitri and Shakti had been assigned to scout a quadrant of Naraka's eastern hunting ground for tiger spoor. They weren't supposed to track or kill the cats, simply observe the traces and report. It was a one- or two-day job, no special rush, but they'd been gone three days when searchers found their corpses gnawed and rotting in the swamp.

Murdered. Shot down by trespassers who would be punished for their crime, once they had been identified.

Naraka knew he couldn't blame their deaths on wildlife officers or soldiers. If the killers had authority, the bodies would have been removed for burial in some detested pauper's cemetery. Leaving them behind suggested that the triggermen were outlaws in their own right, or perhaps involved in some covert agenda that defied Naraka's present understanding.

Poachers?

It was always possible, of course. Naraka's group was not the only gang at work, although it was the largest, strongest and most ruthless. Few of his competitors would risk an overt hostile move against him, but there was a chance that Shakti or Vasitri might have angered rivals they encountered in the field, thus bringing death upon themselves.

In that case, Naraka thought, it should not be difficult to find the men responsible. Some time would be required, but he could speak with local villagers, make inquiries among his rivals, ferret out the ones who acted most suspicious. Barring evidence of a conspiracy against him, punishment would be restricted to the man or men who did the killing.

It was only fair.

The other possibility, however, nagged at Naraka's nerves. If some clandestine operation was unfolding in the Sundarbans, who was the likely target, other than himself? Who was proclaimed in headlines as the nation's most notorious, most-wanted criminal?

No one but himself.

"Take them," Naraka ordered, turning from the corpses toward Jalil Salmalin. "Send someone to find the men who did this. Understand that I want them alive, able to speak."

Salmalin frowned. "We'll look, of course. But I'm not sure—"

"Have them search everywhere, Jalil. Each village. Every hermit's hut. Turn over every log and stone. Interrogate the birds and lizards, if you must. Someone knows something."

"You suspect the military?"

"Not like this. But someone else. Someone who hates us. Hates *me*."

"Why should it be you?" Salmalin asked.

Naraka clutched his first lieutenant's arm, leaned close and hissed into his ear. "Who else is wanted? Who else galls the state as much? Who else warrants a special exercise to root him out?"

"But what if—?"

"Do as I have said!" Naraka snapped, pushing Salmalin away with a force that nearly made his old friend stagger. "Now!"

"It shall be done," Salmalin answered, looking wounded as he turned away and started barking orders at the men.

Naraka had no time to deal with injured feelings at the moment. He was under siege, the only one to recognize that fact so far, and he could not afford to hesitate. Already, unknown enemies might be advancing into striking range. He wouldn't know them until they appeared before him, poised to kill.

Unless Jalil could find them first.

It was a challenge, but he knew the Sundarbans like no one else who hadn't come of age there. Soldiers, mercenaries and assassins were as children in the great swamp, cut off from the world they recognized as surely as if they had been marooned on Mars.

The men who sought to kill Naraka were in *his* world now. And they would not escape alive.

Naraka swore that to himself, an oath of blood.

14

The village had no name, as far as Mehadi or Takeri knew. Bolan approached it with reluctance, while accepting their suggestion that the locals might provide some pointers to Naraka's hideout, even if they didn't do so consciously.

It was a risky game, and Bolan couldn't help remembering that villagers throughout the Sundarbans had either helped Naraka hide from the authorities or managed to ignore him while the ten-year hunt was going on. A snitch in time could have prevented countless murders, wasted man-hours of effort and spared countless animals from being slaughtered on the sly.

But that was part of it, he understood. Naraka killed the tigers that the locals feared and hated. Couple that with bribes, and with the fear of how he might retaliate against a person or a village that betrayed him, and Naraka could effectively control the Sundarbans with only token forces under his command.

In which case, Bolan thought, why am I here?

The answer came back to him, quick and clear: to make it right.

The fact that certain people—even hundreds of them—made their own accommodations with a killer, didn't mean that justice should be set aside or retribution should be waived. It didn't matter if a given segment of the population tolerated or actively approved of certain crimes. There was still a tab to pay, and Bolan had been sent to collect from Naraka.

The village wasn't much to look at, hovels built from mud
and scrap materials, with thatch roofs overhead. The people
had a vaguely unwashed look about them, as if even in the
middle of a swamp, water could not be spared for bathing.
Most of them were lean, with narrow faces, wary eyes and
sour dispositions. A few tried smiles for size as Bolan's team
approached, with Mehadi and Takeri speaking Hindi, but he
didn't trust them for a heartbeat.

"They see hunters from time to time," Takeri told him,
after several minutes of protracted dialogue that Bolan
couldn't understand. "The groups pass through, going this
way and that. Then soldiers come and go, seeking the hunters.
These folk try to stay out of the way."

"Uh-huh." Bolan wasn't convinced.

"The headman," Mehadi told him, nodding toward a griz-
zled ancient, "claims to know Naraka by his reputation only.
Very bad and dangerous, he says."

"Telling us what we want to hear?" Bolan asked.

"Probably. But even if he means it, he may still know
where Naraka camps. The problem's getting him to tell us."

Bolan knew what the problem was. He needed a solution.
"Can you get it out of him?" he asked the woman.

"Perhaps. He's asked if we will honor him by staying for
the evening meal, maybe to pass the night among his people."

Bolan didn't like it, didn't trust the little scarecrow figure
or the others who presumably obeyed his orders, but unless
they tried to milk more information from the villagers, their
whole day would have been wasted. If they couldn't move
among the local villagers and speak to them, the manhunt for
Naraka would degenerate into a hopeless game of hide-and-
seek, with Bolan roaming aimlessly around the Sundarbans,
seeking his quarry under stones and rotten logs.

"I don't trust anything they'd feed us," Bolan told her. "If
they line up with Naraka, they could spike it, poison us or

dope us long enough to take our weapons, get us hog-tied for the slaughter."

"If we stay and do not eat, it is an insult to the village," Mehadi said.

"Better to leave now," Takeri said, "than to stay and make them angry."

Bolan had a choice to make as leader of the team. He understood the risks and thought he had a way around them, for the moment. "Find out what they're having," he instructed. "If there's any kind of roasted meat, we stick to that, as long as we can watch the preparations. Find a way to pass on anything that could be drugged or poisoned."

"Good," Mehadi said. "I can watch the women cook, and talk to them at the same time."

"I'll see if I can get more information from the chief," Takeri said.

And that leaves me the odd man out, Bolan thought, but he couldn't argue with their delegation of responsibility. If one of them could steer the conversation into English, he'd be happy to participate, but in the meantime he was sidelined, left to watch their hosts and search for any sign of trouble in the making.

Bolan let a pair of young women lead him to a tree stump in the shade, but he declined the beverage they offered him, sipping instead from his canteen. Purification tablets only worked on germs, not drugs or poisons, so he wasn't taking any chances with the villagers who might turn out to be Naraka's allies.

Bolan took a chance and asked the girls, "Does either one of you speak English?"

"But of course," the younger of the pair replied. "It is the state's official language, after Hindi."

Bolan knew that, but he wasn't sure the message would've penetrated so far into the mangrove swamps. He asked the second girl, "And you?"

"I speak some English, yes," she said.

He took a chance. "My friends and I are looking for the man who hunts tigers," he said. "Naraka is his name. Does either of you know where we can find him?"

After trading doe-eyed glances with her friend, the older of his escorts said, "It is illegal to hunt tigers in the Sundarbans. We do not spend our time with criminals."

"Of course not," Bolan said, and did his best to match their carbon-copy smiles.

INDRA MEHADI GRUDGINGLY admitted to herself that she was getting nowhere in her efforts to interrogate the women while they cooked. One or another of them shrugged and grunted at her questions, answered some in monosyllables—all negative—and pointedly ignored the rest.

So much for sisterhood.

It was a different world, removed from her experience as if she had been whisked through time and dropped among people who lived before the invention of the telephone, computers, possibly the wheel. She watched them cooking, kept an eye out for suspicious herbs and mushrooms, but the various ingredients they used were mostly foreign to her, unlike anything she'd seen in stores or on her dinner plate.

She recognized wild onions and some kind of squash, but otherwise the roots and greens were all alien. For all she knew, Matt Cooper could be right. The villagers might drug or poison them to win Naraka's favor, or at least to divert his wrath.

Asking about the poacher while the women worked, dropping his name, only evoked a stony silence Mehadi couldn't penetrate. She finally gave up and watched from the sidelines, an observer ostracized. The village headman didn't come to check on her, distracted as he was with questions from Takeri.

All in vain, she reckoned, but perhaps...

Belatedly, she wondered if the villagers might try to warn Naraka while they were in camp. It was a natural response, if they were allied with the poacher, and she wondered now if Cooper had considered it.

Too late, perhaps.

It was impossible to watch all of the villagers at once, and how could they prevent one slipping out, in any case? They couldn't walk into a village and forbid its people from fetching wood or water, dealing with their normal sanitary functions, and the like. In fact, if runners had been sent to fetch Naraka, they were likely on their way—perhaps had reached his camp already if it was nearby.

Mehadi considered that and wondered if it was a bad thing. She already knew that Cooper and Takeri would attempt to keep her out of any action with the poachers. They would not permit her to approach Naraka if they could prevent it. Only through her own initiative could she achieve her goal of vengeance.

And if that meant being captured by the man she meant to kill, so be it.

On the other hand...

She had observed that most of the male villagers were armed with knives. Some would have firearms in their huts, she guessed, for hunting boars and other animals that weren't protected under law. If she could find one of those weapons, somehow claim it for herself, she would be better fixed to greet Naraka when the time came for their final meeting.

How to accomplish that? she wondered.

She couldn't simply walk into the nearest hut, pick up a rifle and expect no one to notice or object. But if she spotted one beforehand, prior to any trouble, maybe she could reach it quickly if the need arose.

And take it with her when they left?

She knew that would require some artistry when she considered the fact that she had no pack, bedroll or coat in which to hide a weapon. If she found a handgun, she could likely hide it underneath her shirt, but she did not expect to find a pistol in the village.

One of the larger knives might make a difference, and they were relatively easy to conceal, but how could she obtain one when the village men all wore them on their belts? In other circumstances, one on one, she might have cast all modesty aside and tricked one of the men into disrobing, but seduction did not strike her as an option in the present situation.

Watch and wait, she thought. If there is need and opportunity, do what you must.

It was the crowning lesson of her life, but it had come too late to save her father or avert her mother's suicide.

Next time, she wouldn't be too slow, too late.

If she was ever close enough to strike Naraka down, Mehadi vowed to herself, she would not hesitate.

But for the moment, she could only bide her time and watch the village women go about their chores. When they were nearly finished with the meal, and the roast pork was taken from its spit, she joined Bolan in his spreading patch of shade.

"Tree stump?" he asked her, as she crouched beside him.

"No, thank you."

"What's cooking?" he inquired.

"The meat should be all right," she said. "They used a little salt, but nothing otherwise. The rest, I couldn't say."

Takeri joined them moments later, kneeling next to Mehadi, boxing her between himself and the American. She could feel him watching her but offered no acknowledgment.

"I'm thinking," Takeri said, "that this may be a mistake. What if one of the villagers has gone to see Naraka?"

"It's a risk we take," Bolan replied. "One reason why I draw the line at sleeping over."

"What if poachers come while we are here?" Takeri asked.

"We deal with them," the Executioner said.

"And the villagers?"

"Their call. If they stay out of it, we do our best to prevent civilian casualties. If they jump in against us, then they've made their choice."

"Here comes the headman," Mehadi told her two companions. "I believe it's dinnertime."

THE PORK WAS SEARED and smoking on the outside, still a ripe and bloody pink within. Aware of trichinosis as a rampant Third World problem, Bolan nibbled only on the crispy edges of his portion, while he smiled and nodded to his hosts like a committed happy camper.

Mehadi and Takeri ate the half-cooked meat more readily, but Bolan wasn't in a mood to criticize. He had enough to do, watching the villagers watching his party, following Mehadi's occasional translations of the running dialogue. A casual observer might've thought it was a cheerful scene, but Bolan felt an undertone of tension stretching from the moment when they'd first approached the village.

"The headman," Mehadi said, "asks me if you enjoy the food."

"It's great," Bolan replied.

"He wants to know why you eat only tiny pieces of the meat."

"Make something up."

"Such as?"

"Tell him I have lactose intolerance."

"He may not understand me."

"Better yet."

The Executioner suddenly noted movement in the huts directly opposite, a group of men who had not joined the feast. From where he sat, Bolan couldn't make out what they were doing, but waited for them to emerge and show themselves by firelight. Balancing a tin plate on his lap and eating greasy pork with his left hand, he let his right drop to the Steyr AUG that lay beside him, never out of reach.

Takeri sat to Mehadi's right, the woman placed between himself and Bolan. As figures started to emerge from the huts across the compound, still beyond the reach of the firelight, Bolan leaned across and told Takeri, "Watch these guys. Be ready if they make a move."

Takeri frowned and nodded. Mehadi was about to question Bolan when he caught a glimpse of gunmetal, poorly concealed by one of the advancing villagers.

With lightning speed, the Executioner discarded his unfinished meal and raised his assault rifle. Mehadi gasped, recoiling, and her backward movement made it easier for Bolan as he found his target. Half a dozen stragglers from the dark huts had weapons in their hands, but they were frozen by the sight of Bolan leveling his rifle at their chief.

The old man raised his hands aloft and started speaking rapidly in Hindi.

"He demands to know why you insult his hospitality," Mehadi translated.

"Tell him I don't like the men with guns, standing behind him. If they make another move, he'll be the first to die."

Her strong voice carried to the ears of every villager around them, stopping those who had begun to stir and shift, as if preparing for a rush against the three outsiders. Apparently, they weren't prepared to risk the headman's life.

Not yet.

"We're getting out of here," Bolan informed his two companions. "Tell them I want all those weapons empty. They have ten seconds, beginning now."

Takeri handled that translation, rising as he spoke and brandishing his rifle. The armed men hesitated, glancing back and forth along their ragged skirmish line, then started to comply. Some pulled the magazines from semiauto rifles, while the others worked bolts and pump-actions, dropping cartridges around their feet.

"All right," Bolan said when that job was done. "Now have them drop the weapons, then pick up the cartridges and magazines. I want the ammunition pitched as far as they can throw it, out into the woods."

"Wait!" Mehadi said, before Takeri could translate the latest order. "I want one of them, with ammunition."

Bolan thought about it. If a fight was coming, which seemed likely, having one more weapon on his side could only help, even if Mehadi didn't qualify for marksman's honors. Scanning up and down the line, he saw three INSAS rifles, two bolt-actions and a pair of cheap pump-action shotguns.

"Fair enough," Bolan replied. "If I were you, I'd take one of the semiautomatics and collect the other magazines that match it. First, tell all of them to take three long steps backward, and remind them what will happen to their headman if they try anything cute."

When every member of the would-be firing squad had stepped back out of lunging range, Mehadi went forward, scooped a rifle from the ground and claimed three loaded magazines. A moment later she was back at Bolan's side, her captured weapon cocked and loaded.

"Now," he said, "I want them to collect the other shells and pitch them off into the woods, as far as they can throw them."

Grumbling accompanied the translation of his order, but the angry gunmen did as they were told. Bolan stood watching cartridges fly toward the tree line, catching firelight as they tumbled through the air. He heard them patter down in darkness, heavy drops of lethal rain.

His final order, Bolan knew, carried the most inherent risk. "Tell the headman to rise and shine. He's coming with us."

Mehadi hesitated. "But—"

"Takeri, tell him!"

Slowly, the headman rose and went to stand before them, while his people stirred and muttered ominously.

"We're heading west," he told Takeri. "Get him started. Indra, stay as close as possible. I'll take the rear. Let's go!"

Takeri drove the village chief in front of him, prodding the older man with his rifle when he faltered. Once beyond the ring of firelight in the village, darkness fell upon them like a cloak, but they knew hesitation would be fatal. They would find a trail or blaze one, but they had to get away.

Mehadi was close behind Takeri. Even without looking back, he knew he hadn't lost her yet. He heard her footsteps, muffled curses when she stumbled, and he half imagined that her scent was carried to his nostrils on the night breeze, even though he knew that was improbable.

He wasn't a bloodhound, had no ability to track another person by her smell, yet it seemed real.

Takeri hoped they hadn't lost the American, their one hope of living through the night ahead, but he couldn't afford to stop and check. If anyone among them had the skill to move through darkness, tracking others, it was the American.

No sounds of gunfire came from behind them, which meant Cooper hadn't been compelled to fight his way out of the village. They were clear, he figured, unless the villagers decided to pursue them.

How? With what?

Takeri reckoned there would be more ammunition in the village, somewhere, maybe other weapons that they hadn't seen. The headman's people had been primed to kill them, or at least to take them prisoner, and that told him that they were working with Naraka. Having gone that far to tip their hand, it followed that they might pursue Takeri's party through the forest, if and when they overcame their fear of harm befalling their chief.

Would fear of Naraka outweigh that concern? Did the

poacher own more loyalty from the rural peasants than their chief? Takeri hoped not, but he wasn't ready to predict how the natives of the Sundarbans would act in any given situation.

They'd been close to death, he knew that much, and his distraction over a woman had prevented him from noticing the villagers as they prepared to strike. If not for Cooper's vigilance, Takeri knew he might be dead, or a prisoner confined pending Naraka's ultimate decision of his fate.

Better to run and fight, he thought, than to be slaughtered like a trussed-up hog.

And soon, Takeri reckoned, he might have that chance.

"Takeri, wait!" Mehadi called out to him in a half whisper.

He reached out for the chief, grabbed a handful of his shirt and hauled him backward. He hissed at him to wait a moment, as the woman caught up with them. "What is it?" he demanded.

"Someone's coming," she said.

Sandwiching the village chief between them, Mehadi and Takeri aimed their rifles back along the track they'd followed westward from the village. It didn't rate description as a trail, but it would likely be apparent to any pursuers, if and when they came from that direction.

Maybe they were coming now.

Takeri let his finger curl around the trigger of his INSAS rifle, sighting down the barrel into darkness. He was just about to fire when a voice called to them, "Don't shoot! It's me."

Takeri started to relax, then felt the tension flood back into him as Bolan said, "They're coming behind me. Look for somewhere we can stop and make a stand."

Looking was problematic in the darkness, with only stray moonbeams to light their way, but Takeri scanned the strange terrain, careful to keep the village chief close by. He wasn't sure if he could shoot the old man, should he try to run away, but in his present mood Takeri knew a swift blow to the head or gut would be no problem.

"Here!" Mehadi said moments later. As they followed her voice, she said, "It isn't much, but maybe good enough."

She'd found a point where two or three trees had collapsed together, possibly after a lightning strike. The tangled roots and branches made it difficult to tell the trees apart, where they lay overlapping one another, but the jumble made a solid bulwark to the left or south of their selected trail.

The four of them had ample room behind that hulking wall, screened by the writhing roots and limbs. It would be difficult for trackers to approach them from the front, and storming their position would be doubly dangerous, obstructed by the jagged upthrust limbs while under fire.

It seemed the kind of place where snakes and scorpions would shelter, but Takeri had no flashlight to detect them, and he wouldn't dare to use it if he had one. Trundling the headman in front of him, he followed Mehadi's lead, with Bolan bringing up the rear.

They took positions on the makeshift battlement, some twenty feet between them as they settled in to wait. Takeri took the length of rope that served as the chief's belt, used it to bind his captive's hands and warned the prisoner that he'd be shot immediately if he tried to flee. The chief shrugged, then sat down and leaned against the nearest massive tree to wait for Judgment Day.

WAITING WAS THE MAIN PART of a warrior's life, the tedium disrupted periodically by savage violence and numbing fear. Mack Bolan had sampled all of it and knew that for beginners, waiting often was the hardest part.

He'd heard the first sounds of pursuit before he'd jogged a quarter mile out from the village. He'd expected them to stall a little longer, thinking of their chief, debating what they ought to do. Instead, it seemed they had begun collecting arms and ammunition right away, ignoring the potential danger to their headman if they followed Bolan's team.

Or maybe they were just supremely confident of their ability to get him back unharmed.

There might be reason for that confidence. This land was theirs, known intimately to the villagers from birth. Where Bolan and his allies had to pick their way along an unfamiliar track, the hunters might be swift and sure, closing the gap with deadly speed. It also stood to reason that a few of them, at least, were decent shots. They had to have been seasoned hunters, or their families would have starved.

So they were coming to retrieve their chief and to avenge the insult to their honor. Over and above that, Bolan reckoned they were working for Naraka—either on retainer, to dispose of nosy trespassers, or in a bid to cultivate goodwill by exercising personal initiative.

In either case, they would outnumber Bolan's team and likely wouldn't hesitate to kill. He knew he needed to surprise them, shock them to their very core, and leave any survivors too dispirited to carry on the hunt.

He glanced back at the chief, reclining stoically in shadow, near Takeri. Mehadi had taken her customary place between them, Bolan having judged that she would be the weakest link in their defenses if the hunters came around their flanks on either side. From where she knelt, she had a clear shot at the trail and any other point along a firing line that stretched for fifty yards or so from north to south.

The only question was whether she could use the rifle she'd been so anxious to take. Could Mehadi bring herself to fire at men, much less find grit enough to kill them? he wondered.

If she froze, it would be dangerous for all concerned, but Bolan meant to let her have one chance. And if she failed at that, he might not have to scold her.

Not if all of them were dead.

Sounds of pursuit were drawing closer. He glanced along the rough wall of their makeshift fortress, noting Mehadi and Takeri straining for a first glimpse of their adversaries in the darkness.

Leaning forward, Bolan told them, "Hold your fire no matter what, until I start the party. We're still trying to avoid a massacre, if possible."

"And if they shoot first?" Mehadi asked.

"Wait for me, regardless," Bolan answered.

"All right," she said, and farther down the line Takeri nodded affirmation.

They were ready—or, at least, as ready as they'd ever be without more time and gear. The Executioner had no mines to plant, no hand grenades to rig as booby traps, with trip wires strung across the trail. Just rifles and the will to use them if the villagers were bent on drawing blood.

The one thing Bolan knew beyond a shadow of a doubt was he couldn't trust them. No matter what they promised to retrieve their headman, it would all be lies. They either served Naraka or were bandits in their own right, schooled to prey on strangers. Either way, Bolan was confident they wouldn't take their chief and leave without a fight.

No problem there.

If it was blood they wanted, then the Executioner was ready to provide it. He would teach his enemies a lesson about taking victory for granted. Even if they killed him here, this night, survivors of the skirmish would remember, and perhaps take something with them from the carnage when they fled.

He hadn't meant for this to happen, but the choice was made. His foes had called the play, but they would not control the game.

Bolan lined up his weapon on the trail and listened to the hunters, careless in their haste. That racket was another costly error. The only question was whether any of the trackers would survive to learn from their mistake.

And whether Bolan would survive to see another day.

15

Abhaya Takeri blinked sweat from his eyes, squinting into the darkness around him, in search of a target. He heard people approaching through the forest, hurrying despite their bid for stealth, and knew the villagers were following his trail. They wanted to retrieve their headman, punish those who'd taken him and possibly win favor in Naraka's eyes.

Takeri glanced back at his prisoner and found the old man still in place, sitting with shoulders slumped, as if asleep. Takeri didn't want to kill him, but his patience was exhausted. If the captive tried to run in the confusion, when the shooting started, he would thereby sign his own death warrant.

It was hot and miserable crouched behind the fallen trees, clutching the INSAS rifle to his shoulder, staring down the barrel into darkness broken only here and there by stray moonbeams. Takeri hadn't noticed the oppressive heat when they were lounging in the village, but it weighed upon him now, after his forced march through the jungle with a prisoner in tow.

Enemies who knew the land were coming for them, and he wondered whether he could do his part to turn them back. Mehadi's apparent confidence embarrassed him, making Takeri feel as if he was the weakest member of the team. That feeling strengthened his resolve, but still he wondered whether it would be enough.

His rifle's magazine held twenty rounds, and Takeri had the fire-selector switch set for 3-round bursts. A bandolier containing ten spare magazines was draped across his chest—more than enough, Takeri thought, to deal with angry villagers and still have ammunition left to face Naraka.

If he lived that long.

A slender shadow-shape appeared before him, rising from a clump of ferns. Takeri framed the target in his sights, caressed the rifle's trigger with his index finger, but refrained in deference to Bolan's order. He would wait, trusting the American to signal when the killing should begin.

More shadows were appearing from the forest, edging closer, hesitating as if some sixth sense had warned them of the ambush. Could it be? Had some clue already betrayed Takeri's team to their pursuers? But if that was true, why did the trackers show themselves at all?

Takeri scanned the line of silhouettes, counting eight, knowing that others doubtless waited farther back in the darkness. For all he knew, the whole village had followed them to save their elder.

How many was that? Takeri hadn't counted when he'd had the chance, but he supposed there had been fifty adults in the village. He wondered if the women would come hunting with their men, then decided that it didn't matter.

Anyone who tried to kill him was the enemy.

Those enemies were edging closer, some of their weapons visible, a glint of errant moonlight here and there on gunmetal. Takeri held his target, measuring the range as it was slowly whittled down. He wondered what was wrong with the leader, if the man had gone to sleep.

Come on, Takeri urged silently. They're close enough!

As eager as he was to hear it, the first shot from Bolan's rifle made Takeri jump and threw off his aim. He compensated swiftly, swung his INSAS rifle toward the shadow-target as it ducked and turned, recoiling from the muzzle-blast, and sent three 5.56 mm rounds hurtling across the chasm at 3000 feet per second.

One of them, at least, appeared to strike the target, though Takeri wasn't positive. He couldn't hear the sound of bullets striking flesh, because a dozen guns were firing all at once, but as he fired, his target seemed to lurch and stagger for a heartbeat, then dropped out of sight.

That could mean anything, he knew. Perhaps the target was unscathed, had merely stumbled on a root or threw himself below the line of fire in self-defense. Takeri had no time to think about it further, as the forest came alive in front of him, winking with muzzle-flashes, echoing with heavy-metal thunder. Bullets swarmed around him in the night, some plunking solidly into the trees that formed his bastion, while others sizzled through the air above his head.

How many guns?

Takeri couldn't stop to count them, had his hands full simply firing back at muzzle-flashes from the tree line, ducking when the bullets came too close, then popping up to fire again. He tried to count the bursts he fired, subtracting spent rounds in his head, but couldn't keep it up. The rifle would inform him when he'd spent his load, its slide locked open on an empty chamber, useless while it waited to be fed another magazine.

And in the meantime, was he doing any good?

The others were returning fire from their positions. He heard no whimper from the woman, only breathless little curses as she ducked and dodged incoming bullets, always coming back to fire again. Takeri felt a sudden, fierce, unreasonable pride in her performance and her courage, but he had no time to analyze the feeling.

He was busy fighting for his life.

Ten endless seconds into the engagement, when he'd

burned up roughly half a magazine, Takeri thought about the prisoner. He turned to check the old man, found him gnawing at the knots that bound his wrists as if he were a snared fox trying to remove a leg.

Takeri watched him for a second, then could spare no more time. Leaning from his position on the leafy barricade, he swung his rifle like a golf club, cracked its butt against the chief's skull and dropped him in a boneless heap.

That ought to hold him for a while, Takeri thought, and turned back to his war.

BOLAN HAD DROPPED his first man with a single bullet to the chest, a kill whatever way they sliced it, fast or slow. The fallen hunter had no face, was just another shadow-form as all hell broke loose along the firing line.

There seemed to be fifteen or twenty weapons firing from the tree line, but it was a rough count and made no allowance for potential flankers slipping through the darkness on their left and right to take them from behind. Bolan supposed he had a minute, give or take, before those shooters found their vantage points, and he would make the best of it.

Takeri and the woman were holding up their end, keeping the enemy engaged. He didn't know if Mehadi had been trained on semiauto rifles sometime in her short life, but she seemed to have a feel for it, conserving ammo when she could have burned it up.

So far, so good—if he considered being cornered and outnumbered "good."

He saw two figures breaking to the right, going for an end run. Bolan tracked them, thumbed the Steyr's fire-selector switch to 3-round bursts and led the forward runner by a yard.

His index finger curled around the trigger, lighter than a lover's touch, and gently squeezed. Three of his remaining bullets sped downrange to meet the moving target, spun him like a dervish in the midst of prayers and put him down.

The second runner saw his comrade fall and tried to veer off course too late. A second burst from Bolan's rifle clipped him on the run and punched him over sideways, vanished into darkness.

Bolan couldn't count on instant kills, but with the 5.56 mm tumbling projectiles any hit was brutal, a potential killer. At the very least, he knew that wounded targets were eliminated from the battle by traumatic shock and blood loss.

Good enough.

Three down, and how many to go?

Too many, right.

The opposition had a motley arsenal of weapons, old and new, including semiauto rifles, slower bolt-actions, and several shotguns. Slugs and buckshot filled the air, rattling the branches over Bolan's head and etching abstract patterns in the heavy mangrove trunks he used for cover. Nothing they possessed could penetrate the giant trees, but if a shooter managed to outflank them…

Someone had to check on that, Bolan realized, and only he had the skill required to handle it. He couldn't just take off without a warning, though, in case his sudden disappearance panicked Mehadi and Takeri. Even if they hesitated only long enough to look for him and question each other, it could be a fatal lapse.

Staying below the line of fire, Bolan moved in to close the gap between Takeri and the woman. Leaning close, he told them, "I'm going out to look for flankers. Hold the line. I'll be right back."

Takeri nodded, turning back toward the firing line, while Mehadi flashed a nervy smile. "Good hunting," she said, then faced forward, squeezing off two rounds in rapid-fire.

Bolan drew back, chose left for no good reason other than

the fact that he'd already dropped two runners on the right and moved in that direction, merging with the shadows at the south end of their barricade.

He traveled in a crouch, letting the sounds of battle from behind him cover any passing noise he made along the way. Ten yards, fifteen, and Bolan was beginning to suspect he'd got it wrong, that no flankers had come in that direction, when a subtle movement in the shadows up ahead caused him to freeze.

Two men—no, make that three—were moving toward him on a collision course. If they had seen him, Bolan knew they would've opened fire already, but their guns were silent. Faceless in the night, they were intent on covering the ground and taking up positions where they could attack his teammates from behind.

It was a good plan, something Bolan might've done himself, but they had blown the opportunity. He'd either stop them, or raise enough hell dying that his comrades would be tipped to watch their flank.

But Bolan didn't plan on dying.

He waited for the gunmen to draw closer. They were walking two abreast, the third man coming on behind the others. He could've taken them already, from a range of forty feet, but the delay allowed him to be sure that no more shooters followed them.

When he was satisfied of that, Bolan peered through the Steyr's optic sight and framed his first mark, aiming for the flanker's chest. Three targets made it challenging, but he was not intimidated. Fear was the farthest thing from Bolan's mind.

A chill had settled over him.

A little closer, said the small voice in his head. Just one more step.

16

The runner reached Naraka's camp an hour after nightfall. Naraka heard the outcry of a sentry on the southwestern perimeter and drew the Browning semiautomatic pistol that he carried in a holster on his right hip, cocked and locked. Naraka's thumb was on the safety, ready to release it, when he saw his men approaching with a stranger carefully surrounded. He let himself relax.

The runner's village had no name, but when the guards described it to Naraka, he knew instantly which settlement they meant. He slipped the Browning back into its holster, waved the sentries back and took stock of their visitor.

He was a young man, winded from his journey, clearly frightened after passing through the swamp alone by night, and worried how Naraka might react to his message. Naraka always tried to wear his best face with the locals, but his temper got the best of him sometimes, when he was disappointed, and the memory of those occasions lingered, passing into local legend.

"What's your name?" he asked the runner.

"Ravi Asad."

"You've traveled far through many dangers, Ravi. Tell me now, what brings you here so unexpectedly?"

"Strangers. In the village."

"Oh?"

"A white man and two others, one of them a woman."

"With an escort?" Naraka asked.

"No."

That was strange—in fact, almost unprecedented, Naraka thought. Smiling with an effort, screening any hint of apprehension from his face and tone, he urged the runner, "Tell me more."

"Our headman makes them welcome," the villager said. "Perhaps they stay the night. I left before it was decided, sir."

"These strangers...were they armed?"

"Both men have rifles, sir, and side arms. They are dressed as soldiers, all in green, but have no rank." A nervous hand brushed Ravi's sleeve. "No patches here."

"What sort of rifles do they carry?"

Ravi glanced around him, at the sentries, pointing toward an INSAS rifle. "Like that one," he said.

So, they were not ordinary hunters who had bribed their way around the mandatory uniformed escort. Some of Naraka's poachers carried military weapons, but they saved them for encounters with police and game wardens, while others scoped four-legged prey. As for the woman...

"What brings them into your village?" Naraka asked.

"When I left they were asking about you."

"Indeed? What did they wish to know specifically?"

"I did not hear it all. The headman ordered me to find you and report."

"I understand. But what you did hear?"

"They asked if you have dealings with the village, if you visit there and if our people know the way to reach you."

"To come here, you mean?"

"Into your camp, yes."

"I see."

And he was starting to, Naraka thought. First, he had two men dead—murdered, in fact—and now came news of armed intruders in the Sundarbans. Obviously unofficial travelers, or at the very least, supposed to look that way. No escort to protect them—or, in the alternative, observe them when they broke the sacred rules.

Naraka understood that kind of thinking. He'd long wondered if and when the government would start to use his own methods against him, but so far, official dedication to the law had kept him relatively safe. Now it appeared someone had thrown the rule book out the window and dispatched assassins to achieve what their police and troops could not.

Only the woman puzzled him sincerely. Her role in the plot, particularly if she was unarmed, eluded him. Naraka never thought of women as combatants—never really thought of them as people, if the truth be told—and he had no idea what she was doing in his wilderness with two men who were plainly sent to murder him.

Of course, he wasn't absolutely positive. There was a small margin of error, he grudgingly acknowledged, but it wouldn't alter his immediate response. Naraka knew what he had to do, and once he had decided, there was no room for debate.

"Jalil!" he snapped, expecting his lieutenant to be close at hand, not bothering to look for him.

"Yes, sir?"

"Take men, perhaps a dozen, and collect these strangers from the village. I hope to speak with them, but if they offer any threat…"

He left the rest unspoken, trusting Salmalin to know his own job.

"And the woman?" Salmalin asked.

"Bring her, if feasible. If not, she's one of them."

"I understand."

The runner had been watching, listening, bobbing his head as they conversed. He spoke shyly to Naraka. "I will guide them back, hoping that I've been of service."

"Nonsense," Naraka said. "My men know the way. You've run a good race and you need to rest. Sit down. Relax. Enjoy some food and wine."

"But I should go—"

"You stay with us tonight," Naraka said. "Jalil will go and see these strangers, bring them back here one way or another. Naturally, if he cannot find them, or if he should walk into a trap, I like to have insurance."

The young man frowned. "I do not understand."

"Do you not? Then I'll explain it to you," Naraka said, with a wolfish smile. "Jalil goes to investigate your story. If the strangers don't exist, or if he should encounter any other difficulty, you will be the first to pay the price for treachery. The first," Naraka added, wiping off the smile, "but not the last."

17

Killing did not provide the sense of freedom Indra Mehadi had imagined she'd feel when she set out on her vengeance quest. And yet, it did not traumatize her, either, as she'd feared it might. She felt no pleasure, she thought, because she hadn't killed Naraka yet. And no uneasiness, perhaps, because the men she'd slain were trying to kill her.

The first was just a shadow, moving forward from the tree line when Cooper had started firing, and she'd done the same, firing twice before the silhouette collapsed. There was a certain unreality about it, fighting shadows, but the muzzle-flashes and the whisper of bullets passing close beside her helped her remember who and where she was, what she was doing there.

This was her second life-or-death encounter since she'd left home to avenge her family against Naraka. First the rapists, then these villagers and yet she was still no closer to her goal. Seeking another target, she told herself she had to survive this challenge for her parents, to eliminate the man who had destroyed her family.

But she knew her survival was not guaranteed.

Matt Cooper had gone off to look for flankers, leaving Takeri and herself to hold the makeshift fort. They were all right, so far, but still outnumbered three or four to one, with bullets swarming through the air around their heads.

She found another mark, her third so far, and fired before she had a chance to think about it. Hesitation could be fatal, she realized, a luxury that she could not afford. Her bullet struck the man, but she knew instantly that it was not a kill shot. He staggered, cursed, then fired his own weapon in answer, pellets from his shotgun coming dangerously close to her face.

She fired again, teeth clenched around a prayer for guidance, fearing that it might be blasphemy. In any case, she scored a solid hit that time, her adversary pitching over backward into darkness, blasted from her field of vision.

To her left, she heard Takeri cursing, cast a glance in his direction and discovered that he'd spent another magazine. Still on her first, she guessed she would run out of ammunition soon, leaving two magazines before she was effectively unarmed.

And what would happen then?

If any hostile villagers were still alive and pressing the attack, Mehadi supposed that she would die.

But not just yet.

As long as she was breathing and had bloody business to complete, she wasn't going to surrender. Not to two men, or two dozen. Not even Shiva the Destroyer would deter her from pursuing her intended target, while she lived.

Off to her right, a gunman broke from cover, charging toward the massive barricade. The move surprised her. He might even have impressed her with his desperate courage if she'd had the time to think about it, but there was no time.

She swung her rifle toward the running man and squeezed the trigger twice. Both hits, she thought, but he kept coming, lurching forward with a snarl of pain and fury. He had almost reached the lower of the two great mangroves, reaching out left-handed for a grip to help him climb it.

Mehadi fired a third time, heard and felt the rifle's slide

lock open on an empty, smoking chamber. If she'd missed her target, there'd be no time to reload before he reached her, scrambling over rough bark in his peasant sandals, leveling his weapon at her face.

But she had not missed. Her final bullet, meant to strike the gunman's chest, had found his throat instead and punched him through a clumsy backward somersault, tumbling away, no longer any threat to her at all.

Ducking below the mangrove parapet, Mehadi removed her empty magazine and slipped a fresh one into the receiver. Cooper had explained to her that each accommodated twenty live rounds, but she couldn't be sure the villagers from whom she took the magazines had kept them fully loaded. Lacking time and opportunity to count her cartridges before the battle, she could only do her best with what she had.

With the fresh magazine in place, she gripped the rifle's cocking handle with her left hand, drew it sharply backward and released it, thankful for the sound that put another cartridge in the chamber. She was ready once again to help Takeri turn the tide.

But where was Cooper when they needed him? she wondered.

Mere moments after he'd told them he would soon return, she had listened to the sounds of gunfire from the swampland to her left. He'd gone in that direction, hunting, and she feared he could be dead, but there was nothing she could do about it. If he was alive, he would return. If not...

Another gunman steeled his nerves to rush the barricade. Mehadi was almost ready for him, missing with her first shot, scoring with the second. As her target crumpled, she could only think of one round wasted, praying that it wouldn't mean the difference between survival and extinction.

Somehow, the storm of hostile fire increased, flaying the mangrove bulwark that protected Mehadi and Takeri. She didn't think that reinforcements from the village had arrived, although she couldn't rule it out. More likely, she decided, those who still remained were massing for a final charge against their enemies, to overwhelm them in a rush, at any cost.

Would it succeed?

Frightened, and yet determined not to show it, Indra Mehadi braced herself for the attack.

JUST ONE MORE STEP, Bolan thought, sighting through the slim scope of the Steyr AUG. His lead target stood rock-still in the shadows, as if waiting, half turned toward the gunman on his left, then shrugged as if in answer to some question Bolan couldn't hear.

The man took the final step.

Bolan squeezed off a 3-round burst from twenty feet, not needing to see the 5.56 mm manglers strike their mark to confirm the kill. Before the first dead man had time to drop, the warrior was already swinging toward the second, sliding into target acquisition with an ease born of long practice and experience.

His muzzle-flash, the crack of autofire, had stopped the others in their tracks. They would've bolted in another moment, but they didn't have that moment. Time was up for both of them.

They simply didn't know it yet.

The second rifleman began to turn, retreating, when he should've simply dropped and rolled. But he didn't have training, simply ran on instincts telling him to get the hell away from there as fast as possible.

But it was already too late.

The second burst from Bolan's rifle ripped into the man as he was halfway through the turn, drilling his shoulder, arm and rib cage. The combination was an instant killer, mangling heart and lungs in a single blinding flash of pain.

The villager made a strangled huffing sound, air driven from his punctured lungs as he went down, gone by the time he hit the ground.

And that left one.

The sole survivor of the flanking team triggered a single shot, then grappled with the stiff bolt-action on his hunting rifle. Whether he was unfamiliar with the weapon or the bolt was rusty, Bolan neither knew nor cared. The fumble bought him precious time, and it was all he needed to complete the triple play.

Three rounds from seven paces, and he'd barely had to aim his weapon. His man went down without a whimper, leaving Bolan as the sole survivor on the field. Behind him, to his right, the sounds of battle still reverberated from the mangrove fortress. His companions were under siege.

Watching for enemies along the way, the Executioner circled to the east, using the path his recent adversaries had blazed through ferns and knee-high grass. Ahead, he saw the muzzle-flashes of the hunting party, winking in the night like giant fireflies, beckoning him.

He was behind them in another moment, noting that the troops were up and on the move. Seven or eight of them, he calculated, forming to hurl themselves against the bulwark hiding Mehadi and Takeri. Bolan trailed them, gaining ground, until the nearest of his enemies was almost close enough to touch.

He never knew exactly what betrayed him to the rifleman. One moment they were traveling in tandem, and the next, his adversary pivoted to face him, leveling a rifle from the hip. Bolan was ready for it, firing as the shooter turned.

At point-blank range, the impact of his bullets plucked the gunman off his feet and slammed him backward, in the same direction he'd been traveling an instant earlier. The other vil-

lagers were firing as they ran, heedless of what happened behind them, so intent on killing that they missed Death running
on their heels.

Before them, Mehadi and Takeri were unloading now with
everything they had, firing at anything that moved, and Bolan
knew he'd simply be another enemy if he pursued the others
toward the fallen trees. Rather than risk a bullet from his own
allies, he stepped behind a tree, using its cover while he started
aiming at the hunters from the rear.

He dropped another and another, watching two, then three
more fall to bullets from the barricade. Even then, the trackers didn't seem to understand that they were caught within a
cross fire, riddled from both sides.

The last three nearly made it all the way. Shoulder to shoulder, racing toward their deaths, they scaled the mangroves, firing as they climbed. Takeri toppled one, Mehadi another. But
the third mounted the summit and triggered one more shotgun blast before a round from Bolan's AUG drilled him between the shoulder blades.

The Executioner allowed the final echoes of gunfire to die
away, before he called out toward the mangrove bastion,
"Hold your fire! It's me. I'm coming in."

"Cooper?" Takeri called out.

"Coming in," he said again, and stepped from cover, passing by the fallen as he crossed the killing ground. When he
got closer, he asked, "Is everyone all right?"

"Not everyone," Mehadi replied.

In seconds, Bolan scaled the barrier and stood beside them.
Neither one of them was injured, but he saw what the woman
meant a moment later. Down below, the village chief lay
sprawled in blood, killed by the gunshots from his would-be
rescuers.

Damn it.

The last thing Bolan had wanted was to tangle with civilians, but the trackers hardly qualified as innocent. They'd chosen sides and paid the price accordingly.

"We need to get away from here," he said, "before the next bunch comes along."

"The next?" Mehadi asked. "From the village?"

"Or from somewhere else. We're in Naraka's backyard now," Bolan reminded her. "Between the villagers and all this racket, let's assume he's on alert."

"What should we do?" Takeri asked.

"Push on," Bolan replied.

18

The village was in turmoil when Jalil Salmalin got there with a dozen of Naraka's men. *His* men, as well, Salmalin tried to tell himself, but even though he wished it true, the feeling was never quite the same.

The first hint of disaster was the wailing cry that had reached Salmalin's ears even before he'd glimpsed the thatch-roofed hovels of the village. Without seeing the source, he'd recognized the sound of women mourning, so familiar from his youth, when every loss from his own village rated a similar display.

It shouldn't be like this, Salmalin told himself. He was supposed to find three strangers dining with the villagers, perhaps already drifting off to sleep. The runner had been sent to warn Naraka and to bring his gunmen here before trouble occurred.

But obviously, something had gone wrong.

Salmalin stopped and sniffed the air, seeking the smell of cordite that hung over shooting scenes, sometimes for hours afterward, but he detected nothing. Only wood smoke and the smells of recent cooking reached his nostrils.

He sent a point man forward to announce them, to make sure that the grieving villagers were not unduly startled. Even though they should've been expecting him, Salmalin feared that in their present state they might seize guns and open fire before they recognized their latest visitors.

Where were the others? Those he'd come to claim?

Salmalin knew there was but one way to find out.

When ample time had passed without gunfire or warnings from his scout, Salmalin led the others forward. Sullen faces met him as he stepped into the clearing. Women wept, while children clutched at them, and the few men he could see stood glaring from the sidelines in an angry group.

Without preamble, Salmalin addressed the men. "What has happened here?" he asked. "You sent for help with strangers, yet I see none present."

"They are gone," one of the men replied, his tone a bitter snarl between clenched teeth.

"Gone where?" Salmalin pressed.

The brooding spokesman pointed vaguely toward the west. "That way. They've murdered many of our best," he said.

Salmalin scanned the small village again, frowning. "I see no bodies. Where are they?

The peasant pointed vaguely westward, as before. "Our headman, Bhaskar Lal, ordered that we should hold the strangers for your master. They surprised us, though, and took him hostage. Twenty of our young men followed them, to punish their impertinence and bring back Bhaskar Lal."

"And they have not returned?" Salmalin guessed.

"A short time later," the villager said, "we all heard shooting in the forest. There." The finger aimed again, at nothing. "When it stopped, a scout was sent to find out what had happened."

"And?" Salmalin was already tiring of the questions.

"He found our young men dead, and Bhaskar Lal, but of the other three, no sign."

"When will you bring them back?" Salmalin asked.

"As soon as we can organize materials. So many bodies, and so few of us remain."

The women wailed again, as if on cue. Salmalin raised his

voice to drown them out. "Before you start," he said, "describe these strangers in as much detail as possible."

"They were two men and one woman," the peasant answered. "One man and the woman were as we are, Indian. They spoke Hindi and English. The other man was white, about so tall." He raised his hand approximately six feet off the ground. "A soldier, that one. But the other man, I'm not so sure."

"Did the white man speak Hindi?" Salmalin asked.

"English only," his informant said. "The others translated for him when we spoke Hindi to them. Both men dressed as soldiers—much as you—but only the white man seemed at ease. He saw us coming for him and blamed Bhaskar Lal."

Which was correct, Salmalin thought, but kept his thoughts to himself. "Tell me about the woman," he said.

"She dressed as a man, no sari," the villager said, with evident contempt. "No modesty."

"And was she armed?"

"She had no rifle when they came into the village, but she took one when they left."

"One of your weapons?"

"Yes. Like yours," the man said, pointing to the INSAS rifle tucked beneath Salmalin's arm. "And three more magazines."

After a moment's thought, Salmalin said, "Take us to see your dead. We may find traces of the strangers and pursue them."

"But, the tigers—"

"Are you men, or children?" Salmalin asked, sneering. "They have murdered twenty of your people, and you fret over a *cat*, when we are here to guard you?"

Shamed, the village men stood muttering among themselves for several seconds, then their spokesman nodded. "I will show you. We can start to bring the bodies home."

"Do as you please when we are finished," Salmalin said. "Now, prepare and let us go. Hurry!"

Ten minutes later, when a dozen of the village males had gathered guns and cutting tools from their respective huts, the party set out, marching westward. Salmalin was secretly delighted to have the peasants lead the way. Not only would they guide him to the spot he had to examine, but they'd also frighten any tigers from the path—and draw fire if the strangers heard them coming through the forest.

If the strangers had not fled.

Salmalin, in their place, would have been busy making tracks, but he could not speak to the motives of three people he had never met. A white man, possibly a soldier, marching with two Indians—and one of them a woman who had armed herself for war.

It was strange and troublesome.

Jalil Salmalin couldn't wait to see what happened next.

19

It was approaching midnight when the Executioner decided it was safe to camp. They'd gone at least four miles beyond the battle site, and he didn't believe any pursuers from the village would come looking for them where they were.

And where were they, exactly? he wondered.

Bolan hadn't brought a mobile GPS device, knowing the mangrove forest would prevent him from obtaining uplinks to the necessary satellites. Instead, he had his compass and dead reckoning, buttressed by Mehadi's "sense" that they were heading in the right direction for Naraka's camp.

They had reached a stream where they could purify the water with tablets to replenish their canteens, while standing watch in turns and catching up on some much-needed rest. There'd be no fire, but with the pork he'd eaten in the village still a lump in Bolan's stomach, he was quite willing to go without a midnight snack.

"I'll take the first watch," Takeri said. "I won't sleep in any case."

"You can't go days on end without it," Bolan said, though he had done precisely that on numerous occasions.

"Do not be concerned. I'm fine."

Bolan decided not to argue. After checking out a corner of the clearing with his penlight, he spread his poncho on the ground and laid his pack down as a pillow. Prior to resting, he said, "We need to talk about tomorrow."

"Yes," Mehadi replied. "It must be better than today."

"Don't count on it. Naraka's camp won't be a pushover, assuming we can find it. And if he gets word of what went down tonight, he'll be on full alert," Bolan said.

"Searching for us, perhaps," Takeri said.

"I wouldn't rule it out. From this point on, we can't afford mistakes."

"Have we made one so far?" Takeri asked.

"The village, maybe," Bolan answered, careful not to look at Mehadi as he spoke. "But, then again, we had to try something. We didn't make them hit the panic button. That's down to Naraka."

"No more villages," Mehadi said. Speaking from her space in the clearing. "Please."

"Not that way," Bolan promised. "If we have to tap another one for information, we can try another angle. Maybe send Takeri in alone."

"Oh, yes?" Takeri made a sour face. "Thank you, so bloody much."

That got a laugh from Mehadi, even making Bolan smile.

"Okay, then. Maybe not. I'm hoping we can find Naraka's people on our own, from here. Or maybe they'll find us," Bolan said.

"They will outnumber us," Takeri said.

"But we have the advantage of surprise."

"Unless they see us first!"

"Be sure they don't," Bolan replied. "Your life depends on it."

"I am aware of that," Takeri said. "It doesn't help."

"I'm hoping it will keep you on your toes."

"What will we do," Mehadi asked, interrupting, "when we find Naraka's camp?"

"I'll have to scope the layout," Bolan said, "before we hatch a plan."

He wasn't sure how much to share with Mehadi and Takeri, even though he trusted them. Ideally, if and when he found Naraka's camp, Bolan would slip inside and tag the poacher, raise as much hell as he could with other members of Naraka's team and leave the site unharmed, without a tail.

At least, that was the ideal plan, but those were hardly ever realized. In fact, it had been his experience that something nearly always happened to upset the perfect plan—human error, possibly an "act of God," as some insurance companies preferred to call it—or a dose of plain bad luck.

"We'll watch our step tomorrow," Bolan said, as he lay down, pulling the Steyr AUG against his chest. And to Takeri, "Wake me in three hours. I'll take over until dawn."

"No worries," Takeri replied.

Before he closed his eyes, Bolan saw Mehadi bundled in Takeri's poncho, turning so her back was to the clearing. She had yet to speak about the firefight or the men she'd killed, and Bolan hoped it wouldn't be a problem for her—for the rest of them—while they were searching for Naraka.

Maybe her desire for sweet revenge would get her through it, casting those who'd tried to kill them with Naraka. And why not? As Bolan told himself again, the villagers had chosen sides and forced his hand, before he ever made a hostile move against them. If they hadn't tried to take his party prisoner, he never would have bagged their elder as a hostage, and the others would still be alive. They'd picked the game and lost it. Bolan wouldn't lose sleep over fighting them on their own terms.

But he knew the young woman would probably be different. Underneath the cool exterior, she might be hurting for the men who doubtless would've killed her if she hadn't dropped them first. It made no sense, in terms of logic, but survivor's guilt was a phenomenon that Bolan understood. Some soldiers grieved for fallen comrades, wondering why they'd survived when friends had fallen all around them. Others mourned the men they'd killed in battle, as if each had snatched small pieces of their souls and carried them away.

Bolan lived daily with the ghosts of friends and foes alike, but they did nothing to detract from his performance in the world of flesh and blood. They were a part of him, as ingrained as the color of his hair and eyes, but they did not control his actions or his destiny.

As sleep reached out to claim him, Bolan hoped the ghosts would let him pass the next three hours without bloody dreams.

INDRA MEHADI WAITED until Cooper was asleep. She judged it by his breathing, fearful that she'd wake him if she turned to stare at him. Takeri was the problem, standing watch and ready to wake Cooper in three hours. He had promised not to fall asleep.

And yet…

Mehadi had seen the way he'd stumbled on the trail, leaving the firefight, as they fled to find a safe camp site. She sympathized with him. Her own fatigue was amplified by the exertion of the march and battle, by the trauma she'd experienced while killing men and nearly being killed herself.

It wasn't as she had imagined, aiming guns and firing into human bodies. In her rage, of course, she'd only pictured killing one man, pausing long enough to let him know the reason, see the glint of fear and possibly repentance in his eyes before she pulled the trigger. She had considered that she might be forced to neutralize Naraka's men, as well, but that lay in the realm of fantasy.

Ideally, she would face Naraka by himself, with no one else around to stop her. She would have him in her power, bound or held at gunpoint, while she lectured him on how he'd ruined her life. Whether he wept and begged or sneered at her in stark defiance, the last act of her mental drama always ended the same way, with her slitting Naraka's throat, or shooting him, or clubbing him until his mother wouldn't recognize his face.

Regardless of the means, she had her revenge.

Her parents, then, could rest in peace.

She was on the verge of that goal, had already learned the art of killing, but she feared that Cooper and Takeri would preempt her. They had reasons of their own for snuffing out Naraka's life—political, whatever—and while she knew she should have been relieved to have experts perform the task, instead she feared that they would cheat her of the one thing she could do for her late parents.

How else could she honor them in death, except by personally spilling the blood of her father's killer?

She lay and waited for an hour, slipping closer to the edge of sleep herself and fighting back from it, until she reckoned it was safe to turn and watch Takeri. He was nodding in the darkness, plainly sleepy, though he'd promised to remain alert. His body would betray him yet, she thought.

But would he fall asleep in time?

She had to go before Takeri woke the tall American, for Cooper wouldn't sleep on duty. She was sure of that, and he would catch her when she tried to leave the camp.

It was essential that she slip away from them, finish her quest alone. It was for that reason she'd come into the Sundarbans, and she would not be foiled by strangers, even if they'd previously saved her life.

Naraka was her problem. He had killed her father and driven her mother to suicide. Indra knew about his other crimes, the dozens—even hundreds—he had murdered, but she didn't care. Nor did she care about foreign diplomats and tourists who'd be better off staying home. In avenging her parents, she would pay the debt for all of those Naraka had assassinated through the years.

He could die only once, and she meant it to be by her hand.

Watching Takeri nod, she eased her poncho back, slowly and carefully sliding out from underneath it. Rising to her feet was risky, knowing that her knees or ankle joints might pop and rouse the sleepy watchman. Even reaching down to get her rifle was an exercise in jangled nerves for she feared that Takeri would wake up and ask what she was doing, thereby rousing Cooper from his sleep.

And what if they should catch her at it? Would she fight them? Hold the pair of them at gunpoint while she fled? Mehadi had no illusions about being able to elude Matt Cooper in the jungle. She might outwit Takeri, but the tall American would track her, overtake her and disarm her if he wanted to.

Unless she stopped him first.

That could mean killing him, and Mehadi wasn't sure she could accomplish that even if she was so inclined.

She had the rifle now, and her last spare magazine protruding from the left hip pocket of her denim jeans. Takeri's shirt hung loosely on her, soiled with dirt and perspiration. No great loss, she thought, in case he never got it back.

She retreated slowly, alternately watching Cooper and Takeri, while she checked the ground behind her, planting each foot carefully to minimize the sound. Reaching the nearest tree, she slipped behind it, grateful for the cover, and began to move a bit more rapidly. Still careful, though, in case her crashing through the forest woke the sleeping men.

Takeri would catch hell from Cooper, over sleeping on the job, but that was not her problem. She was free from interference now, ready to carry out the mission that had brought her to the Sundarbans. Ready to kill Naraka for the pain that he had caused her family.

If she could only find his camp.

JALIL SALMALIN HAD BEGUN to wonder if his guides had any clue where they were taking him. It seemed to him that they had walked at least five miles, but Salmalin supposed that apprehension might influence his sense of time and distance. If they didn't reach the so-called battleground within the next fifteen to twenty minutes, Salmalin promised himself that he would—

"Here!" one of the villagers called back to him.

Salmalin started pushing past them, followed by his hunters. He was rushing when he stumbled on the first corpse, literally, and one of the peasants caught his arm to stop him falling facedown in the dead man's blood.

Salmalin pulled away, righting himself without a word of thanks, and used his flashlight to illuminate the body. Shot twice, from the look of him, the dead man had apparently collapsed while running toward a pair of fallen mangrove trees that formed a natural redoubt, some ten to fifteen yards ahead.

Salmalin swept his light across the killing ground, spotting more corpses as the beam ranged here and there. He didn't bother counting, merely noting that the dead men he could see had all been shot while moving toward the mangrove barricade, intent on reaching it and those who had concealed themselves behind it.

Enemies. Still nameless, faceless. Still at large.

Salmalin picked his way around the dead, avoiding outflung arms and legs, discarded weapons. When he reached the tumbled mangrove trees, Salmalin first looked for a way around them, then decided it was simpler just to climb. Passing his flashlight to his nearest soldier, with the INSAS rifle slung across his back, he began to scramble up and over, feeling somewhat as the dead men had to have felt before the bullets cut them down.

Except that no one tried to kill him as he climbed.

Salmalin reached the top, stretched out his hand and caught the flashlight that was thrown to him. He played its beam along the rugged parapet, where cartridge cases glinted in the light, then scanned the shadowed space behind the fallen, interlocking trees.

A single corpse lay waiting for him there, an old man dressed in peasant garb. His hands were bound, the blood that stained his shirt already drying crisp and dark. From the expression on his face, Salmalin couldn't tell if Bhaskar Lal had been surprised by death, or if he'd simply taken it in stride.

Of those who'd brought him to this place, no trace beyond spent brass remained. His trackers might find footprints when the sun rose, something that would let Salmalin follow those he sought, but for the moment they were out of reach.

And if they got away...

He didn't want to think about that, feared to contemplate Naraka's wrath if he returned without the strangers. It was unlikely that Naraka would demand his life—unlikely, although not impossible—in payment for such failure. More probably, he would be fined, perhaps stripped of his rank, some other member of the company promoted to second in command.

The insult rankled, even though it hadn't happened yet. Salmalin fumed at the humiliation, knowing that he had to do something to redeem himself.

But what?

He couldn't wish the strangers back or wave a magic wand and make them suddenly appear. He couldn't even track them until daylight let his scouts begin to search for footprints or any other spoor the interlopers may have left behind. Naraka's patience would be tested, if Salmalin wasn't back in camp by dawn, but if it took more time to find the enemies he had been sent to capture, what else could be done?

His hunters had begun to fan out through the trees, checking the shadows as a measure of security, while their companions from the village set about the grisly business of collecting corpses. If they made litters, Salmalin calculated they could drag home six or eight at once, perhaps be done with it in two round-trips. Say noon the next day—or was that today?

Thankful that it was not his job, Salmalin was descending from the mangrove barricade when echoes of excited shouting startled him. He almost fell, then caught himself and scrambled down the last few feet to solid ground, tugging his rifle from its shoulder sling.

More shouting, and he recognized the voices of his men, but their tone was almost jovial. Moving to meet them as they came back through the trees, Salmalin saw two of his men dragging a third between them, struggling feebly. Only as they closed the gap did he discover that the captive was a woman.

Sudden hope surged through him. Rushing forward, he met the hunters and their prisoner along the way. His men were chattering together, unintelligibly, until Salmalin demanded silence.

Pointing to one, he said, "You. Tell me plainly, who is this?"

"I don't know. We caught her back there." Waving vaguely behind them. "With this!"

The hunter held a rifle in his free hand, while his own was slung across his back. Salmalin smiled, beginning to relax.

"You're just the lady I've been looking for," he said. "Now, if you'll tell me where to find your two friends, we'll be on our way."

20

Bolan woke to a rough hand on his shoulder, snapping instantly from dreamless sleep to consciousness. His right hand closed around his rifle, his left gripping the arm that shook him, even as he recognized Takeri's face.

It didn't feel like Bolan's time, yet, but before he could consider it, Takeri blurted out, "She's gone!"

"Gone where?" Bolan asked, rising from his poncho in a single fluid motion.

"Gone," Takeri said again. "I don't know where. I—"

"How'd this happen?"

Even as he posed the question, Bolan knew the answer. Mehadi couldn't have escaped their campsite if Takeri had been on the job. He'd either wandered off or gone to sleep, in either case allowing her the opportunity to slip away.

"I'm sorry," the Indian said, his shoulders slumped in shame. "I felt no drowsiness at first, but then...."

"Never mind. It's done," Bolan said. "What we need to think about is where she's going."

"She will try to kill Naraka."

"Her rifle's gone, I take it?"

"Yes," Takeri answered.

"All right, then," Bolan said. "We have two choices. We can let her go and hope she doesn't ruin everything, or we can try to intercept her."

"Bring her back against her will?" Takeri asked.

"Not back," Bolan replied. "We have nowhere to keep her, and we're still hunting Naraka. If we track her down, we'll either have to take her with us or eliminate the threat, once and for all."

"You don't mean.... No." Takeri shook his head. "I can't. I *won't*."

"Your call. But if Naraka's bags her, there's no telling what he'll do to make her talk. She won't hold out for long, and when she tips him off, his people will be ready for us."

"We must help her, then!" Takeri said.

"If you can track her in the dark, then let's get started," Bolan answered, but Takeri simply shook his head again.

"I cannot," he replied.

"Then we can't move until sunrise. Collect your gear, and let's be ready for first light."

There was no point in chastising Takeri for his failure on the watch. He recognized his error and clearly regretted it, punishing himself beyond what any words from Bolan could achieve. Their task was to locate Mehadi or to find Naraka's camp before she did.

Before she ruined everything.

Bolan did not believe in second-guessing choices and events he couldn't change. Rescuing Mehadi from the men who would have raped and killed her was a choice that he did not regret. He'd do the same again for any innocent who crossed his path, yet Bolan's act of mercy was the spark that lit a fuse he couldn't sever. It was burning now, beyond control.

And the explosion might destroy him.

He didn't blame Mehadi for the compulsion to avenge her parents. Something similar had launched his private war against the Mafia. The fact remained, however, that her quest for vengeance jeopardized his mission and his life, as well as Takeri's.

If she found Naraka's camp before he did, there was no doubt in Bolan's mind that she would try to kill the poacher. Possibly emboldened by the skirmish she'd survived, Mehadi might feel that she was up to handling killers who had dodged the army and police for years on end.

But Bolan would've bet that she was wrong.

If she was killed outright, before she reached Naraka, then a portion of his problem would be solved. At least she couldn't talk, in that case, but he also had to think about survivors from the village where they'd stopped, assuming that they would communicate at some point with Naraka.

Either way, Bolan knew he was running out of time.

Once his intended target was alerted to the impending danger, Bolan knew Naraka would take measures to protect himself. Whether that meant moving his camp or fortifying it, launching patrols or taking off for parts unknown, the Executioner couldn't begin to guess.

The only thing he knew for certain was that he was on Naraka's turf, with one ally against two dozen adversaries, give or take. The more time that Naraka had to prepare himself for the assault, the worse off Bolan's team would be.

Surprise had been their edge, but he could feel it slipping through his fingers now. Between the villagers and Mehadi, Bolan guessed that any hope of true surprise was nearly blown.

To salvage anything, at this point, would require both skill and luck, with an emphasis on luck.

He sat and watched for daybreak, barely tasting the dried beef that was their meager breakfast, washed down with tepid water from the canteens. It made a poor meal, but Bolan couldn't guess when they'd have time to stop and eat again. Maybe that night, maybe the next day.

Maybe never, if their luck ran out.

"It's light enough, I think," Takeri ventured sometime later.

"Light enough to try, at least," Bolan replied.

"Please understand—"

"Forget it," Bolan interrupted. "It's behind us now. Watch out for what's still waiting up ahead."

21

Dawn was breaking when a sentry woke Balahadra Naraka, murmuring apologies together with the news that Salmalin's patrol had finally returned to camp. Naraka kept them waiting while he dressed, then shaved his cheeks and chin around the thick mustache that made his WANTED posters so distinctive.

Finally, he left his tent and found Salmalin sitting in his camp chair. He watched his first lieutenant leap upright as his master appeared. Salmalin's haste drew snickers from the men surrounding them, all quickly stifled as Salmalin scanned the ring of faces with an angry glower.

"I have news," Salmalin said, when his dignity was recovered. "And a prisoner."

Theatrically, Salmalin snapped his fingers, and two hunters pushed past others who had hidden them, dragging a woman to the forefront of the crowd. She struggled in their grip but could not break away.

"This is the woman from the village," Salmalin said.

"I can see that from her clothes," Naraka answered. "Were you forced to kill her male companions?"

"No, sir."

"Ah. Then bring them forward, and stop teasing me."

"We don't have the men."

Naraka noted how Salmalin's tone had changed. At first,

it was *I* have a prisoner, and now, *we* missed the men. The shift bespoke a certain weakness in Salmalin that would bear close watching in the future. If he was afraid to take responsibility, how could he lead?

"Tell me," Naraka said.

Salmalin told the story of their night march to the village and their subsequent diversion to the site where better than a dozen villagers lay dead, gunned down by still-unknown intruders who kidnapped the village chief. While they were examining the dead, searching for clues, the woman seemingly appeared from nowhere, lost and wandering, as if intent on being captured.

It was quite a story, featuring Salmalin as the star. Naraka watched the other members of the search team while Salmalin spoke, noting each time they smirked or grimaced at some deviation from the facts as they recalled them. He expected some embellishment of any such adventure, but Naraka had to wonder whether Salmalin was entirely worthy of his trust.

At last he frowned, deciding to postpone consideration of that question to another time. He had the woman to interrogate and her companions were still at large, roaming about the forest armed and obviously dangerous.

Looking for him.

That was the part that most intrigued Naraka. It was clear to him that someone feared or hated him enough to put professional assassins on his trail. Soldiers, police and game wardens had proved themselves incapable of capturing him, and now the big guns had arrived.

But were they any good?

Naraka gave his enemy points for slipping through the first trap, in the village, and for killing those who tried to run them down. It showed a certain ingenuity and courage, but the trackers had not proved themselves.

Not yet.

As for the woman, she remained a mystery—one Naraka planned to solve that very day.

His first approach was open and direct. "Who are you?" he inquired. "Who sent you here, and why?"

The woman answered swiftly, "Indra Mehadi. I'm a writer for the *Hindustan Times*. I came to get an interview with India's most-wanted fugitive."

Naraka smiled. "An interview?"

"She carried this," Salmalin interjected, holding out a rifle for his leader to inspect. Naraka made a show of studying the weapon, though he did not touch it.

"A gun and strange companions," Naraka said. "Curious activities indeed, for a reporter."

"I was carrying a camera and tape recorder," she replied almost indignantly, "but they were stolen by two men who tried to rape me in the forest. Probably they would have murdered me, but two more strangers came and shot them first. They forced me to accompany them."

"Did they molest you?" Naraka asked.

"No."

"Instead, they gave you this?" He nodded toward the rifle that Salmalin held.

"I took that for myself," the woman said, "after the people of a nearby village tried to capture us. The two men who had rescued me then took the village headman as a hostage and prepared to leave. I obviously couldn't stay behind. I took the gun from one of those they had disarmed, for self-defense."

"And used it later, I believe," Naraka said.

"That's right." Her tone was now defiant. "Many of the villagers pursued us. Tried to kill us in the forest. What would you have done?"

"I would have razed the village while I had the opportunity," Naraka answered with a smile. "But that's just me."

The woman strained once more, in vain, against the hands that gripped her arms. "Now, if you don't mind, I would like to get that interview," she said.

Incredible.

Her courage stirred Naraka as no other woman had in years. It was a pity that he couldn't trust her any more than his own two arms could hurl an elephant.

"What then became of your companions?" he inquired. "They were not with you when you met my men."

"I left their camp while they were sleeping," she replied. "To find you on my own."

"Simply to talk?"

"And share your thoughts with readers throughout India. Some think you are a hero of the people, others that you are a monster. Most still can't decide."

"And what is your viewpoint?"

"That may depend on whether you intend to kill me or provide the interview," she said.

Naraka had to laugh at that, and some of his hunters joined in. Salmalin did not seem to find the quip amusing, but his sense of humor clearly needed work.

"Unfortunately," Naraka said, as the moment passed, "I fear that you are lying to me. Before we speak of other things, I must first satisfy myself that you are not a liar. So, it seems, *I* must conduct the interview."

"SHE'S GOING BACK THE WAY we came," Takeri whispered. "Why would she do that?"

Examining the trail by dawn's gray light, Bolan had no definitive response. "She might be looking for a reference point," he said, "to find Naraka's camp. Or, then again, she could be lost."

"I vote for lost," Takeri said. "Her knowledge of the area is no better than my own."

"We don't know that for sure," Bolan replied. But he suspected that Takeri was correct.

"If we keep on this way, we'll soon be at the fallen trees," Takeri said. His tone revealed no great enthusiasm for an instant replay of their firefight in the woods.

"The only other option is to cut her loose," Bolan said.

Takeri thought about it for a moment, seeming weary in the pale light as he shook his head. "We can't do that."

"Okay." Bolan nodded and began to forge ahead. It didn't take much skill, since Mehadi hadn't tried to hide her tracks. While she'd blazed a slightly different trail than the three of them had covered, fleeing from the mangrove firefight, she was definitely headed back in the direction of the killing ground and hostile village.

Why?

Bolan supposed that being lost would answer all the questions preying on his mind. Mehadi had left the camp in darkness, trying not to make a sound, and in the process she'd become confused about directions. On the flip side of that coin, maybe she'd thought she had an angle on Naraka's camp and doubled back to find another jumping-off point that made sense to her.

In either case, the tracks they followed had her moving steadily toward danger as the sun rose overhead. If she met the villagers, she was likely to be shot or lynched on sight. They wouldn't try to capture her alive, this time, if they had any sense at all. Or maybe, if they somehow managed to disable her, a slower death would lie in store for the young woman, payback for the slaying of the village headman and so many others.

Indra Mehadi would find no mercy in the hearts of the rural peasants after she had helped to kill their chief, their husbands, sons and brothers.

When they had backtracked to within a hundred yards of

the previous night's killing ground, Bolan found other trails converging on the one they followed. It seemed at least four people had collided, struggled, then retreated toward the fallen trees where he, Takeri and Mehadi had confronted their pursuers hours earlier.

Takeri saw it too, and asked, "What happened?"

"Somebody grabbed her here," Bolan said. Stooping, he searched the ground for bloodstains or spent brass. Instead, he saw only more footprints, leading back in the direction of their makeshift barricade. "They took her this way," he explained, pointing.

"Alive?"

"There's no sign she was harmed, but I can't swear to it."

Together, they crept closer to the too-familiar site, planting each step precisely for the maximum in stealth. Takeri needed no reminder to be quiet. If more trackers had been here, it meant the battleground had been examined, either by surviving villagers or someone else. Some of the searchers might still be around, encouraged by Mehadi's return to the crime scene. And Bolan didn't plan to wind up in the bag as she had.

Not if he could help it.

Twenty yards brought them within sight of the giant fallen trees. A lone lookout was seated on the topmost trunk, smoking, a rifle braced across his thighs. He scanned the tree line lazily, failing to notice Bolan and Takeri in the shadows. Bolan noted that the chief's corpse was no longer lying where he'd fallen in the battle, but he couldn't tell about the rest.

He leaned in toward Takeri and said, "The cleanup detail's been here. They could be coming back for more."

"We can take this one," Takeri whispered through clenched teeth.

"Too much open ground," Bolan replied. "We'd have to shoot him, and there may be others we can't see from here."

"What, then?"

"Stay here. Stay low. I'll circle the perimeter and see what I can figure out."

Takeri nodded, albeit reluctantly, and settled on his haunches, eyes fixed on the smoker forty feet away. Bolan moved out, a gliding shadow in the forest, circling cautiously around the clearing on a clockwise path that took him northward.

He found the trail five minutes later, trampled ferns and grass betraying where a troop of men at least a dozen strong had passed on from the killing ground, away to the northeast. He couldn't tell if Mehadi was among them, from the jumbled footprints, but he knew they hadn't gone back toward the village, and he made an educated guess that they would not surrender the one hostage who might have some information they could use.

He doubled back and found Takeri, still fixated on the lookout. Bolan closed the gap to whisper distance, telling him, "I found the trail."

"She's with them?"

"It's a gamble. Either follow them or head back to the village."

"No," Takeri echoed his own thoughts. "They wouldn't let the peasants have her."

"Right, then. If you're ready, let's move out."

22

"Do what you will," Mehadi challenged Naraka and his men. "I cannot tell you what I do not know."

"Alas," the poacher replied, "in order to believe you, I must satisfy myself as to precisely what you do know."

"I've already told you everything," the woman insisted.

"If that is so, then please accept my most heartfelt apology for the discomfort you must now experience."

The thin smile on Naraka's face belied his gentle words. He stood before Mehadi and to her left side in a claustrophobic hut where the only furniture consisted of a hand-hewn table. Mehadi occupied the tabletop, spread-eagle, with her wrists and ankles bound securely to its legs. Still fully dressed, she eyed Naraka and his two sour-faced companions from an awkward angle that cramped the muscles of her neck and shoulders.

That was nothing, she supposed, compared to the pain she would endure soon.

Ironically, she had already told Naraka almost everything she knew about Matt Cooper and Abhaya Takeri, withholding only their names. She'd said the men had never introduced themselves to her, a small lie that allowed her to suppress feelings that she'd betrayed them to Naraka. And, in fact, she didn't know where they'd come from, who they were working for, or where they might have gone that morning, after learning that she'd fled the camp. Naraka figured they had to be searching for him, but she simply didn't have the answers that he sought.

She would be tortured for speaking truthfully, and when at last she spilled the names—a small and unimportant secret—then Naraka would feel justified. She knew he would demand more suffering to see what else she had withheld from him, and only with her dying breath would he be satisfied that there was nothing more to learn.

But if he didn't kill her, if she managed to survive the ordeal facing her, there was a chance—one in a million maybe less—that she would be released and still have time to snatch a weapon from her tormentors, turn it against them and exact her vengeance.

She would hold on to that hope.

"If you have something else to tell me," Naraka said, "then by all means, please...."

It was too late, she realized, to offer names. Having already lied in that respect, her change of heart would only make Naraka more suspicious. He would certainly mistrust her when she swore to him that names were *all* she knew about her two recent companions. She had doomed herself and could think of no way to repair the situation.

"At what point," she asked Naraka, "will you finally be satisfied that I know nothing more?"

The poacher shrugged. "Who knows? I have an instinct for such things, but no two cases are the same. A few more questions, possibly. Perhaps your dying breath. I cannot say."

The other option, she decided, was to lie outrageously, make up whatever details came to mind and hope the fabrications bought her time, sending Naraka on a wild hunt to confirm her tales. It was a long shot, but it couldn't damage Cooper and Takeri. If it freed her from the table, gave her any chance at all to reach Naraka with a weapon or her own bare hands, it would be worth the risk.

The problem was not to break too quickly. Having stalled this long, Mehadi knew it would be suspicious if she simply crumbled into panic. She had to let the bastards go a little farther, make it more convincing when she pleaded for mercy and began to spin her lies.

"Alas," Naraka said, "you leave me no choice in the matter. Here we have a simple but effective tool for breaking down resistance to interrogation. I became familiar with it in my period of penal servitude, and it impressed me so much that I've applied it to selected representatives of the exalted government for many years, ever since my escape."

Naraka gestured toward an object on her left, and Mehadi turned her head in that direction, straining for a brief glimpse of the hand-cranked mechanism, mounted on a flimsy metal frame with wheels. Electric cables sprouted from the top of it, fitted with dangling alligator clips.

"It is, as you surmise, a hand-cranked generator. Fuel is scarce here in the Sundarbans, but muscle power never fails. The voltage generated is not fatal," Naraka said, "but I promise you that it is quite excruciating. All the more so when applied to certain…tender areas. Will you not speak?"

"I've told you everything," Mehadi replied.

"So sad." He turned to his men. "Strip her."

This was the moment she had dreaded—one of them, at least—as two of the appointed bullies tugged and tore at her clothing, ripping off the buttons of her borrowed shirt. They had a problem with her jeans and panties, since her legs were splayed and bound in place. Confused, they asked Naraka for instructions, and he waved them away angrily.

"It is enough," he said, moving to stand beside the table. Frowning like a connoisseur selecting cuts of veal, he pointed with a knobby index finger. "Fasten the electrodes here…and here."

One of the men retreated and came back with the cables, grin-

ning as he flexed the dull jaws of the alligator clips. When they
were poised above her naked chest, Mehadi released a heartfelt
sob of fear and said, "No, wait! I'll tell you everything!"

TAKERI FOLLOWED BOLAN through the forest, punishing himself with every step for Mehadi's jeopardy. If he had only
stayed awake during his watch, he could've stopped her from
escaping—pinned her down and bound her, if it was required.

But what, then?

They had not come all this way to babysit a woman neither one of them had ever seen before. In that respect, it struck
Takeri as ridiculous, their mission being sidetracked by a total
stranger's plight.

And by your negligence, the small voice in his head reminded him.

During his military service, Takeri knew he would have
been punished for sleeping on duty. In wartime conditions, if
it had resulted in damage or harm to his comrades, he might
have been shot. He was surprised, then, that the American had
made no more of the egregious lapse in discipline, which had
permitted Mehadi to escape.

Escape.

Perhaps that was the key, Takeri thought. She hadn't been
kidnapped while he was dozing. She had left them voluntarily, no doubt in pursuance of her private vendetta against Balahadra Naraka. If Takeri had been wide awake and caught her
leaving, what would the result have been?

More conflict on their team, no doubt—but then, what?
Would the mission have been sacrificed while he and Cooper
played nursemaid to a woman? Would they have returned
empty-handed to Calcutta, with nothing to show for their efforts except some dead peasants?

And would it be a bad thing if their mission failed?

Takeri had not been enthusiastic from the outset. Even

though he recognized Naraka's evil and agreed that someone ought to stop the poacher, why should it be him? Before the outset of this mission, he'd been paid primarily for information, now and then some undercover work with militants, but nothing in the killing line.

Takeri didn't want to earn a reputation as a mercenary for hire. He craved excitement, sometimes, but he didn't need the kind that led to bloodshed—most particularly when the blood was his. It might be helpful, he thought then, if Cooper found the woman and returned her to Calcutta, writing off his quest to find Naraka in the Sundarbans.

Takeri did not think that was the tall American's intention. He believed that the man meant to go ahead, whether they found Mehadi or not. How that would be accomplished was a question that Takeri couldn't answer. For the moment, he could only follow orders and refrain from agitating his comrade by some other act of foolish negligence. The less hostility between them now, the better.

If he failed again, Takeri feared that the big man might dispose of him and push on by himself. The man was capable of that, he realized, although his present fear might be irrational.

Why test it, either way? he figured.

The trail was no worse than the others they had followed for the past—what was it? Two days? Three? He reckoned this had to be their third day in the Sundarbans and wondered how long he'd survive alone, if he was separated from the grim American.

The odds were worse now, he decided, than when they'd begun their quest. Aside from poachers, tigers, snakes and crocodiles, some of the local villagers would also kill him if they had the chance, and he supposed the word would spread quickly. Between Naraka's propaganda and the stories of survivors, skewed to cast Takeri's party as the villains of the piece, they might be judged, convicted and condemned by strangers who had never seen them, much less heard their side.

No matter. They would be avoiding villages whenever possible, for the remainder of their sojourn in the Sundarbans—unless, perhaps, the trail of Mehadi's captors led them to another one.

Takeri asked Bolan what he meant to do if the woman had been captured by the people of a second village, rather than Naraka's men, and Bolan replied, "Let's wait and see what happens."

Wait and see.

Takeri couldn't argue, since his negligence had put them on this trail to start with, but he knew that they were being sidetracked from their main objective.

Then again, if they had to fight, perhaps it would be easier against more villagers, rather than poachers and assassins who had spent the past ten years skirmishing with soldiers and police.

If they rescued Mehadi from another hostile mob, Takeri believed Cooper would still push on to find Naraka. The rescue would only be a detour, distracting him no longer than it took to deal with the impending threat and get his bearings once again.

What bearings?

Therein lay the problem, since they didn't have an inkling of Naraka's whereabouts. Their first plan, wheedling information out of local villagers, had blown up in their faces, leaving them with no Plan B, unless Naraka's men had—

The big American raised a fist in front of him, a silent signal for Takeri to stand still. Takeri thought he saw his companion sniffing the air, and then his nostrils caught a whiff of wood smoke on the breeze.

The Executioner stepped backward, leaned in close and whispered in Takeri's ear. "We've got a camp or village up ahead. Stay here, while I go and check it out."

Takeri nodded his agreement, and a moment later Bolan vanished into the undergrowth and shadows, seeking out the enemy.

A HUNDRED YARDS of swampy mangrove forest lay between the spot where Bolan left Takeri and his final destination. Camp or village, they had something on the fire, the smell of roasting meat wafting to Bolan's nostrils as he closed the gap, one cautious step after another.

He was following the trail of Mehadi's captors, still uncertain whether they were poachers from Naraka's band or members of another village, but his instinct told him it was probably the former. Why would neighbors of the village he had visited want Mehadi in their village?

It made sense if Naraka's men had come along—or if they had been summoned by a village runner—and arrived in time to capture the young woman on the trail back toward the killing ground. Bolan still leaned toward the opinion that she had been lost, a city girl who found the battle site a second time by accident, or possibly by instinct, homing on a place where men with guns were congregated, breathing cordite with their oxygen.

In any case, his trail craft told him Mehadi would be found somewhere within the camp or settlement that lay in front of him. In which case, he would...what?

Give up the mission for her sake if she was being held by local peasants rather than Naraka's gang? Risk his life and Takeri's one more time, to help a woman bent on chasing private vengeance to the point of suicide? What would it cost him if he simply turned away, left Mehadi to her fate?

Bolan covered the last forty yards at a snail's pace, creeping through the sodden forest, placing every step precisely for the minimum of noise. He studied shadows for a hint of human form; watched carefully for traps; tested the breeze for the familiar scents of sweat, tobacco or gun oil; listened for voices, coughing, clanking metal—anything at all.

By slow degrees, the camp revealed itself to Bolan. He heard muffled voices first, becoming louder as he neared their

source. They spoke Hindi, which Bolan couldn't translate, but
at least it let him gauge the distance to his target.

Thirty yards from ground zero, he saw the sentry. A lone
youth stood at ease against a backdrop of exotic blooms and
ferns, making no effort to conceal himself. Bolan could easily have dropped him with a pistol shot, but silence was im-
perative. That meant he either had to sneak around the lookout
silently, or take him down without alerting any of his comrades to the fact.

Clutching the AUG, Bolan began to work his way around
the sentry, circling wide to pass him unnoticed on his left side,
Bolan's right, and moved on toward the camp.

It wasn't large, as such things went, but there was ample
room for twenty-five or thirty people. The accommodations
were a mixed bag, tents of various descriptions standing side-
by-side with huts constructed out of anything available. A fire
pit had been excavated in the middle of the camp and it was
smoking, while two men tended something that resembled a
side of beef.

Elsewhere around the camp, Bolan saw armed men walking, talking, smoking, cleaning weapons. If the place was on
emergency alert, it didn't show. There was no evidence of
hasty preparations to repel attackers, no last-minute drills or
hectic repositioning of riflemen. Naraka's campsite—if, indeed, it was Naraka's camp—revealed no evidence of any
great excitement whatsoever.

Watch your step, Bolan reminded himself.

Before he went to fetch Takeri, Bolan needed to be sure
that Mehadi was somewhere within the camp. That done, he
also hoped to spot Naraka, satisfy himself that they had
reached the end of their rough trail. He circled warily, watching for guards along the way and meeting none.

When he had finished half a circuit, Bolan saw the plywood
door of one hut was open, two men passing through it into

sunlight. One of them he recognized from photos in his dossier as one of India's most-wanted man, the poacher, kidnapper and murderer he'd been sent to eradicate.

Behind the men, as the flimsy door swung shut again, he also caught a fleeting glimpse of someone lying on a table, possibly tied down. He couldn't see a face, but even from a distance Bolan saw the shirt splayed open, and he knew the captive was a woman.

Grim-faced, he suppressed an urge to rush the camp alone. Slowly, carefully, he began his backtrack to the point where he had left Takeri waiting in the jungle.

23

"Stay here. Don't fire until I do," Bolan whispered to Takeri. "After that, you're on your own. Use common sense."

Takeri nodded. "Do not fear that I will fail you."

Bolan squeezed his shoulder and replied, "It never crossed my mind."

He didn't linger with the Indian for any more conversation. They had watched Naraka's camp together for the best part of an hour, charting the erratic movements that supplanted anything resembling an orderly routine. Men wandered here and there, engaged in conversation as it moved them, left the compound and returned.

In all that time, no one approached the hut where Bolan had observed the female captive. That was problematic, since she could've been removed and taken to another hut or tent while Bolan backtracked, found Takeri, briefed him and returned. She could be dead, her throat slashed, carted off into the forest, but at least there'd been no gunfire from the camp.

At one point, they had watched Naraka cross the compound, duck into a tent on the far side, then exit and return to his apparent quarters on the west side of the camp. They could've shot him then and fled, but both agreed that they should take the extra risk, find out if Mehadi was alive and help her if they could.

If it turned out that she was dead, at least they could raise hell among the poachers. Teach them something new about the dangers of guerrilla warfare.

Payback was a bitch, and no mistake.

Leaving Takeri at his post, Bolan circled the camp's perimeter until he reached a point directly opposite the hut where he'd observed the female prisoner. It was as close as he could get, some forty feet, without emerging from his cover in plain sight of every gunman in the camp.

Daylight was not his friend, but neither Bolan nor Takeri had been willing to sit back and wait for nightfall. Indeed, at one point he had thought Takeri might rush in alone, without reconnaissance, but hearing that he might endanger the woman had restrained him.

Stealth had carried them as far as it would go on this, a risky daylight smash and grab. They couldn't creep into the camp, as night would have allowed, and even if Takeri could have passed at first glance for a member of Naraka's outfit, Bolan never would.

It would be blood and thunder when the flag came down, and Bolan only hoped their play wouldn't result in Mehadi being killed before they had a chance to reach her.

If they were too late, then Bolan would complete his mission to the best of his ability, get out alive if possible and add another soul to his expanding gallery of ghosts.

Takeri's role was to provide a critical diversion, circling around the camp, unleashing fire from various positions to encourage the belief among Naraka's gunmen that they were surrounded. He was waiting for Bolan's signal, and that required a move on the warrior's part that could jeopardize his bid to rescue Mehadi from the prison hut.

He had to fire the first shot, and he had to do it soon.

His only edge was that the first shot wouldn't be expected, and the odds against someone pinpointing its precise location were extreme. As soon as he heard the shot, Takeri would start blasting from the far side of the camp, distracting Bolan's opposition while he made his move.

It would've suited him to drop Naraka with the first shot, but the bandit leader hadn't shown himself since Bolan and Takeri had glimpsed him briefly almost forty minutes earlier. Naraka had remained inside his quarters, out of sight, and Bolan couldn't wait for his next glimpse of the prime target. If the shooting didn't flush Naraka out of hiding, he'd be forced to think of something else.

He scanned for targets, found two poachers standing near the fire pit in the center of the camp and framed one in the rifle's sights. The outlaw's magnified profile was swarthy, animated in apparent argument. Bolan had no idea what he was saying, and he didn't care.

The trigger stroke was gentle, sending death downrange at 3,185 feet per second. Bolan delayed just long enough to see his target's head explode, then heard Takeri's rifle stuttering across the camp. At that, he burst from cover, knees pumping like pistons as he sprinted for the prison hut.

The first shot had surprised most of Naraka's men, while the immediate response from Takeri's weapon drew them toward the west side of the camp. One who responded to the shooting was a chunky older man who stepped out of the prison hut, just as Takeri fired his second burst.

The poacher had no trouble spotting Bolan, as the Executioner was running headlong toward him from no more than thirty feet away. Naraka's soldier didn't have a rifle with him, but he wore a long-barreled revolver of uncertain vintage tucked beneath his belt. At sight of Bolan, the gunslinger tried his fast draw, grunting what could only be a Hindi curse as the front sight snagged on his belt.

Bolan shot his adversary in the face without allowing him to draw his gun. The dying man collapsed in an untidy heap, and Bolan leaped across his fallen body, hoping that Takeri's fusillade would mask his single killing shot.

He reached the prison hut, its door ajar, and slipped inside. It took only a heartbeat for the Executioner to see his worst fear was realized.

Mehadi was gone, and he had no idea where they would find her in the camp.

Assuming she was even still alive.

NARAKA AND SALMALIN were deciding on a schedule of patrols, hunched over maps inside Naraka's tent, when gunfire echoed through the camp. They heard one shot at first, immediately followed by an outcry, then repeated bursts of automatic fire that seemed to issue from a new direction.

Abandoning the maps, Naraka snatched a rifle from his bedroll, while Salmalin drew a Browning semiautomatic pistol from the holster on his hip. Salmalin, as befit a good subordinate, went first as they prepared to leave the tent.

Outside, they found the camp plunged into chaos. Men were running aimlessly, while bullets flew among them, dropping runners here and there. Naraka crouched, making a smaller target of himself, and tried to peg the source of gunfire, but he found it difficult. The first few bursts, he could have sworn, had come from somewhere to the east, but then the locus shifted, bullets spraying from another quarter, tearing into huts and tents.

Because the sun was high, Naraka couldn't count on muzzle-flashes to reveal the enemy, and even sound was suspect in the forest, more particularly since his own men had begun returning fire. His ears rang with the shooting, and the echoes kept Naraka from determining how many hostile weapons were involved. It might have been an army.

Or it might be only two.

Salmalin voiced the thought before Naraka could. "Perhaps it is the woman's friends," he said.

"You mean the strangers who first rescued, then abducted her?" Naraka countered. "I am thinking the same thing."

"John Smith and Taj Kalari," Salmalin said, stating names the woman had provided as she spun her story of intrigue.

"Perhaps," Naraka said.

Although he didn't fully trust the woman or the names she'd finally confessed, her story had been plausible enough for him to base short-range defensive plans upon it. But it now seemed that he would not have time to implement those plans.

"We must control the men," Naraka said, "before they start to kill one another. And discover where the hostile fire is coming from. If there are only two men, then they must be moving, changing places. Otherwise..."

Naraka didn't have to finish his thought. If there were more than two men firing on the camp, it meant they were surrounded.

But by whom?

There'd been no shouted warning, no bullhorns or helicopters that would indicate a raid by the police or military forces. Firing from the jungle by surprise was a guerrilla tactic—one Naraka often used himself—against the government's patrols. It would be clever of them to try it, but because Naraka thought them stupid, he could not believe it to be true.

"I'll take the east side of the camp," Salmalin said, and left before Naraka could respond. The heavy firing had been concentrated in that area, so far, and it was best to organize the men there, first, before their surprise became a rout.

Naraka was torn between two options. Instinct told him he should take the west side of the camp and bring his men under control before they panicked. Still, another part of him wanted to grill the woman one more time, find out if she'd expected this attack and kept it from him under questioning.

He'd been too lax with her, that much was evident. Naraka vowed that he would not repeat that grave mistake.

Clutching the INSAS rifle to his chest, Naraka rose and ran

across the compound, ducking bullets as he sprinted toward the tent where he had left the female captive under guard.

TAKERI WAS RELIEVED when the shot was fired at last. The tension coiled inside him suddenly exploded through his rifle, spitting 3-round bursts into Naraka's camp. Instead of being frightened, after so much anxious waiting, the onset of battle came as a relief.

Takeri's first shots winged a poacher sitting on the ground outside a small tent, knocked him on his side and left him thrashing on the ground. Takeri wasted no more bullets on the wounded man but swept on, seeking other targets, anxious to create as much confusion as he could.

He could not erase the thought of Indra Mehadi, lashed to a table, stripped of clothing, doubtless so Naraka's men could torment and molest her. Rage suffused Takeri, blotting out all thought of what she might've told the poachers about Cooper and himself.

What difference did it make? The fight was on. Naraka had not stopped them in the forest, and he'd never have another chance.

Takeri fired again, another hit, then rose and fled along the tree line to his left, while gunmen near his first nest sprayed the woods with panic fire. When he had cleared a dozen yards, Takeri stopped and sought another target. He fired two bursts into a group of poachers milling nervously around the fire pit.

Fire and run. The pattern Cooper had devised to make one man sound like an army, while the other tried to rescue Mehadi from captivity. Takeri had been on the verge of asking for that job himself, but realized before he spoke that he would make a mess of it, most likely sacrificing the woman and himself. Cooper was better suited for such things and definitely wouldn't let emotion override his common sense.

Three bursts, and now he had a choice to make. Should he

continue on or double back, the better to confuse his enemies? Both moves had their advantages and risks, but there was no time for debate between Takeri and himself.

He ran clockwise, twenty yards, while bullets raked the trees and undergrowth behind him. Flopping down behind an ancient log, he scanned the camp for targets and thought he caught a glimpse of Cooper racing toward the hut where Mehadi was confined. It was enough to give Takeri hope and help him choose a mark as gunmen rallied to his side of the compound.

One of the group seemed to be shouting orders at the rest. Takeri recognized him as the man they'd seen before, walking and talking with Naraka while they were examining the camp. Some kind of second in command, perhaps, and all the more important to Naraka in a pinch.

Takeri sighted on the shouting man, was taking up the trigger slack when from his left another poacher ran into his field of fire. It was too late to call the bullets back. They flew downrange and drilled the runner, one of them at least a through-and-through that spattered his initial target with a crimson spray.

At first, Takeri thought he'd hit both men, but the agility of his intended mark as he recoiled and ran for cover banished any such idea. Takeri chased him with another burst, three bullets wasted as the fleeing gunman threw himself headlong behind a squat, ramshackle hut.

Takeri cursed, deciding it was time to double back and run a counterclockwise circuit of the camp's perimeter. Rising, he almost stepped into a bullet that passed close enough to let him feel its slipstream on one cheek. Takeri ducked, seeking the sniper, but no special gunman was revealed.

A stray, then. Nearly lucky for the shooter, even though he'd never know it.

Taking greater care, Takeri ran back toward the point where

he had loosed his first shots on the camp, using the larger trees for cover, sprinting in between them as the firing shifted toward his latest vantage point.

There'd been no time to see if Cooper reached the prison hut or made his way inside. Takeri hoped the tall American could rescue Mehadi, but he had no way of checking in, no means of communication while the battle raged. That was an oversight he'd have to live with, if he could.

Assuming that another lucky shooter didn't drop him in his tracks.

Until that happened, though, Takeri meant to keep on firing, moving, helping Cooper any way he could. They had no signal for the conclusion of the firefight, so he knew he'd have to work it out himself.

Seeing Naraka dead would do it, better still if he could fire the fatal shot. But failing that, Takeri vowed that he would keep on fighting to the bitter end.

24

Mack Bolan spent precious seconds checking out the prison hut. The table with its straps revealed bloodstains, but they were old, ingrained, dried to a rust brown. Nearby, a hand-crank generator rested on a battered dolly, but when Bolan grazed its alligator clips and cables with his fingertips, he found them cool. A sniff and closer look revealed no evidence of scorched flesh on the clips.

Mehadi had been there, he was certain of it, and at least a portion of her clothing had been ripped away, but Bolan couldn't tell what else had happened to her. And he didn't know where she had gone from there.

Somewhere in camp, he guessed. She had to be.

Unless they killed her. Dumped her in the swamp while he was gone.

Before his mind kicked into vengeance mode, Bolan knew he had to search the camp—a task that would be expedited with Naraka's help. Of course, that meant he had to find Naraka in the middle of a firefight, but at least he'd seen the poacher walking to his quarters and could recognize the tent, located on the west side of the camp.

Three strides brought Bolan to the doorway, still ajar. He peered outside, then ducked back as three gunmen sprinted past the hut, pausing a few yards farther on to blaze away with automatic weapons toward the tree line. Bolan wondered if they had Takeri spotted, but the trio turned immediately after firing, racing off in yet a new direction that had no apparent correspondence with their former line of fire.

Panic was spreading through the camp, and that was good for Bolan—to a point. It kept his enemies off balance and disorganized, but it could also spell the end for Mehadi, if Naraka judged her as more liability than asset. Bolan might've doomed her with his first shot, but he couldn't let his mind go there.

Not now.

Somewhere outside the camp, Takeri would be fighting for his life, buying the time Bolan required to look for Mehadi and Naraka. Bolan refused to let defeatist thinking undercut that sacrifice.

He stepped out through the doorway of the prison hut, crouching, plotting a course across the camp. He couldn't see Naraka's tent from where he stood, but knew the way to reach it—if a sniper or a stray round didn't drop him first.

Bolan attacked it as a football problem with a whole new set of rules. He had to reach the opposition's end zone, while defensive players tried to kill or maim him. Bolan could respond in kind, but he was still badly outnumbered, eight or nine to one by his rough estimate.

"Okay," he muttered to himself, and broke from cover in a rush, running a zigzag pattern through the middle of the camp. Bullets sizzled around him, some closer than others, but he didn't get the feel that anyone was really firing at him yet.

That changed as he approached the fire pit, where a couple of Naraka's men appeared to rise up from the earth itself, blocking his path with weapons raised. The grim expressions on their bearded faces mingled fear with rage, but Bolan couldn't guess which one was dominant.

He ducked, dodged, felt the muddy ground slip out from underneath his feet and turned the fall into a saving grace. As the matched set of would-be killers started shooting, Bolan dropped below their line of fire, rolled over once and came up blasting with his Steyr AUG.

His first three rounds punched through the shooter on his right. The dying man crumpled to his knees, then toppled over on his side.

The other took a heartbeat to correct his aim, but by the time he got it right, it was too late. Bolan had stitched him with a rising burst across the chest and lower face that spun him and dropped him in a flaccid heap.

Shaving the odds.

Bolan leaped to his feet and ran toward Naraka's tent. Some of the bullets flying past him now, he guessed, were meant specifically to bring him down. He dodged them, finding cover where he could, steadily pushing on.

When he was nearly there, a poacher rushed at Bolan from his left, armed with a machete that he brandished overhead. The screaming man swung the long blade at Bolan's face, forcing the Executioner to backpedal and shoot him from the hip. Gut shot, the madman dropped his knife and clutched his stomach, then turned on his heel ran off wailing through the camp.

Madness.

A moment later, Bolan stood beside Naraka's tent. He didn't hesitate and ducked through the flap before another enemy could interrupt him. He was ready with his rifle for anything the bandit leader might decide to throw at him.

He found himself inside another empty nest.

The realization had barely sunk in when bullets started ripping through Naraka's tent from two sides, shredding fabric and hissing through the air around his head.

THE FIRST GUNSHOTS startled Indra Mehadi, who was lying in a small tent twenty feet from where Naraka slept. Two of the poachers had brought her there after she spilled her fabricated story for Naraka, answering his questions with a mixture of the truth and total fantasy that seemed to sate his curiosity. They'd marched her through the camp, arms bent behind her back so that she couldn't close her ruined shirt, then bound her hand and foot and left her huddled on the ground without a sleeping pad.

She'd guessed that they would kill her soon, if she was fortunate, but now something had happened to upset Naraka's little world.

She thought at once of Cooper and Takeri. Had they followed her somehow? Or had the army tracked Naraka to his lair? Perhaps a rival band of outlaws had a score to settle with the king of poachers?

Anything at all might help her, Mehadi realized, as she began to struggle with her bonds. She thought the rope around her ankles might be loosening a little, but before she had a chance to test it, guns were firing all around her and a bullet drilled her tent, passing within a foot of where she lay upon the ground.

Frustration wrenched an angry sob from her throat as she strained furiously at the knots that pinned her wrists behind her. Thinking that her teeth might do the trick, she wrestled to contort her supple body, first raising her legs, bent with the knees against her chest, then doubling over so her hands could slip around her buttocks.

For a moment, she was contorted painfully, bound wrists trapped in the crook behind her knees, but then she straightened her legs, knees flattening her breasts, and slowly worked her numbing fists along her calves in the direction of her ankles.

She was poised there, lying on her back, shirt splayed and falling off her naked shoulders, feet up in the air, when someone rushed into the tent. Gasping, she toppled over on her side and felt a cramp sink agonizing claws into the muscles of one thigh.

Fighting the pain, she barely recognized Naraka crouching over her. Wild eyes devoured her, glinting with equal parts of lust and agitation.

"You are trying to escape, I see," Naraka said. "All right, I'll help you."

As he spoke, a dagger suddenly appeared in his left hand. The blade vanished from sight, behind her hip, and Mehadi braced herself for pain that would eclipse the cramp and leave her screaming out the final moments of her life.

Instead, the warm steel passed between her wrists, severed the rope that bound her hands, then moved down to her ankles and released those bonds as well. Before she could relax or make a move, however, she felt its sharp edge at her throat.

"Now you are free," Naraka said, "but only to my purpose. You may come with me or die. The choice is yours."

Mehadi considered it. An hour earlier, facing the generator and its alligator clips, she would have chosen death without a second thought. Now, with her hands free and Naraka's camp under attack, she thought there might be some advantage to survival.

She might even find a chance to spill Naraka's blood before he took her life.

"I'll go with you," she said, and offered no resistance as Naraka hauled her to her feet. He put the knife away and aimed at her with an automatic rifle.

"One false move," he warned, "and I shoot you just like any other animal."

Mehadi ignored the threat and asked, "Where are we going?"

"Out," Naraka said, and shoved her roughly from the tent, onto the battlefield.

DUELING WITH GUNNERS he couldn't see would be a futile waste of energy and ammunition, Bolan realized. They had him pinned inside the tent, perhaps surrounded, tearing it apart with autofire, but to survive he had to make his way outside.

All right, then.

Ducking toward a case of hand grenades that lay beside Naraka's sleeping mat, Bolan palmed one and pulled the pin. A heartbeat later, he was rushing at the tent's back wall, firing a vertical burst that opened a flap in the canvas for him to pass through. As he hit the flapping wall, Bolan flipped the grenade over his shoulder, leaving it behind, and plunged into daylight on the other side.

Four seconds on the clock by then, and it was long enough for two poachers to hear his gunfire, guess his plan and run around behind Naraka's tent to head him off. Bolan was scrambling for distance, down on hands and knees, when they arrived. As they lined up their shots the frag grenade exploded in a smoky thunderclap, spewing its shrapnel through the ragged remnants of the tent.

Bolan rolled with the shock wave, flipped onto his back and was ready with the AUG if either of the men who'd meant to kill him still had any inclination to pursue the matter. Both of them were down, one blowing crimson bubbles through a new vent in his chest, the other on all fours and picking shrapnel from his forehead.

Bolan gave the second one a head shot, dropped him in a heap, then vaulted to his feet and rushed to cover in the shadow of a nearby hut as thunder rocked the camp.

His best guess was that the grenade explosion had set off some kind of chain reaction with the others in the crate he'd seen. The rapid-fire explosions sounded like a string of firecrackers on some demonic giant's Independence Day. Deafened, Bolan could feel the shrapnel ripping through the hut that shielded him and smell its thatched roof burning where the superheated shards of metal came to rest. Screams echoed through the camp as poachers felt the bite of flying steel.

Crawling, the Executioner gained distance from the epicenter of the stuttering explosions, shielded for the moment from his adversaries by the added tumult in the camp. Over the ringing in his battered ears, he wondered about Mehadi and Takeri—where they were, if either one of them was still alive and capable of self-defense.

Gunfire continued in the wake of the grenade explosions, but he couldn't judge directions well at first, as the blast concussion took its toll.

Bolan's immediate priorities remained the same: locate Naraka and find out from him where Mehadi was.

When Bolan glimpsed the two of them together, suddenly, he feared it was a trick of his imagination, maybe something shaken loose by the grenade explosions from a wishful-thinking corner of his brain. A second glance removed all doubt, however.

He was looking at Naraka, prodding Mehadi toward a tent with a rifle at her back.

Bolan stood to follow them, and just as suddenly saw half a dozen of Naraka's soldiers rushing toward him, their faces contorted by snarls. All six were armed with rifles and were firing as they charged him, trusting more to luck than skill in their enthusiasm for the killing moment.

Survival in a firefight hinges on split-second decisions. Bolan knew his targets were escaping, and he couldn't do a thing about it while the six advancing gunmen blocked his path. A lucky hit from any one of them would put him down. Collectively, they had a better chance of killing him than Bolan did of dropping them. He had no cover close at hand, no more convenient stockpiles of grenades or other secret weapons that would tip the balance in his favor.

Fight or flight. It was the choice that had confronted humankind in danger situations from the dawn of time.

Playing for time, the Executioner squeezed off a parting burst and ran.

25

Jalil Salmalin triggered three fast shots into the forest, then re-treated to the cover of a small hut on the east side of the camp.

"What are you shooting at?" one of his hunters asked, wide-eyed and trembling as he clutched an automatic rifle to his chest.

Salmalin had no answer for him, since there'd been no clear-cut target. He'd seen something flitting through the shadows, guessed that it might be a man, and poured his cruel frustration through his weapon into empty space.

"Get ready," Salmalin said. "Check your weapons."

Five men huddled on the west side of the hut, more human flesh than it could cover in the circumstances. All of them were hunched like trolls, eyes flicking here and there around the camp as gunfire crackled, bullets hissing past them from all sides. It was a miracle that none of them was wounded yet, but that would likely change within the next few seconds—and they knew it.

Salmalin had accomplished part of his assignment from Naraka. While he hadn't managed to control and organize all poachers on the east side of the camp, he'd grabbed these five and bullied them into submission while the battle raged around them, led them to the point where they were huddled now, to launch a thrust against their enemies.

Salmalin's observations told him there were gunmen in the

trees along the camp's perimeter. He'd glimpsed their muzzle-flashes, traded shots with them, but doubted that he'd scored a hit so far. They were elusive and fleet-footed, obviously schooled in jungle warfare, forcing him to wonder who they were and why they'd picked this moment to attack.

The woman had to be part of it, he thought. From the moment of her appearance in the nearby village, through the massacre that followed and the firefight now in progress, she had brought the worst of luck to everyone she met. Her male companions still remained at large, although Naraka now believed he knew their names, and it would not have stunned Salmalin to discover that they were among the raiders who surrounded him right now.

As to the why of it, Salmalin was prepared to wait until he had a chance to question a survivor of the raiding party, or to pick the pockets of their dead. And if he never learned the answer, that was fine.

As long as he escaped to hunt another day.

"Ready!" Salmalin commanded.

Glancing at the faces of his five reluctant fighters, he could see that they were anything but ready. Still, he reckoned they would do as they were told, particularly since the ingrained fear of his wrath and Naraka's outweighed any fear of sudden death.

The punishment for cowardice might last for hours, even days, before oblivion released an offender from his agony. The five who crouched before him now had seen it happen and would not have forgotten.

His plan was simple: rush the woods, kill anything that moved in front of them, then pivot to the left or right—it hardly mattered which—and drive the enemy before them to their deaths.

Assuming they could find the enemy, and that they weren't cut down within the first few yards.

Salmalin felt his courage failing, knew that it was time to go before the others saw him weaken and lost all respect for his authority.

"Attack!" he snarled at them, with a grimace to match his tone.

The five leaped to their feet and charged around the hut, toward the tree line, all firing as they ran. Salmalin could have let them go without him, but he rose a heartbeat later and ran after them, afraid to face Naraka's judgment if the effort failed for lack of leadership.

At first, it seemed they would succeed. His men were halfway to the trees and gaining ground, their storm of bullets flaying trunks, ferns, vines and waist-high grass. No one could stand before such deadly fire. The enemy would break and scatter, making easy targets as they fled. Salmalin would—

The man on his far left went down, blood flying from his head. He fell with arms outflung, as if to hug the earth, his weapon cartwheeling through space.

The four survivors turned instinctively to rush the unseen sniper, blitzing him with automatic fire. Salmalin was impressed by their coordination under stress, would have congratulated them if there was time or opportunity.

And then, the second fell. He seemed to trip, then wallowed through a clumsy shoulder roll and didn't rise again. Salmalin saw blood pumping from the chest wounds that had cut him down.

He hadn't seen the shooter, though, and that could be a problem. If—

The third of his guerrillas gasped a cry of pain, staggered and clapped his left hand to his face while dropping to one knee. Salmalin gaped at him, saw dark blood pulsing from between his fingers and the blank look on the poacher's face before he toppled forward, slack and silent.

Two men were left besides himself, and they were turning

now, panic etched deeply on their faces as they fled. Salmalin couldn't blame them, but he shouted at them anyway.

"Stop where you are! Advance!"

They paid no more attention to him than if he had been a gnat buzzing around them, but it hardly mattered. Salmalin saw the muzzle-flashes from their enemy, too late, as short bursts found the runners, drilled them from behind and brought them down.

Salmalin raised his rifle, fired a long burst toward the point where he had seen the muzzle-flare, then did the most outrageous thing that he could think of in the circumstances.

He charged.

His brain was screaming at him, logic telling him he was an idiot, but honor called upon him to succeed where his five men had failed. He had the bastard spotted now. It would require no special skill to cut him down.

The blow beneath his heart caught Jalil Salmalin in midstride, with both feet off the ground. It spun him like a top and brought him crashing back to earth with stunning force, the air punched from his lungs on impact.

As he tried to draw another breath, Salmalin realized that he had lost control over his body. There was no great pain to speak of—he was mostly numb, in fact—but it was no less frightening for that.

Sprawled on the turf, gasping to heaven like a fish out of water, he lay watching as the darkness lowered, then swallowed him alive.

AN ANGRY FLIGHT of bullets rattled above the Executioner as he threw himself behind another hastily constructed hut. It offered him more cover than a tent would have, but it was all a matter of degree. The walls were rusty corrugated metal, echoing from bullet strikes as if he'd crouched behind a giant kettle drum.

A glance told Bolan that he'd nearly emptied out the AUG's transparent plastic magazine. He switched it for a fresh one, braced himself, then did the last thing—he hoped—his adversaries would expect.

Instead of looking for another place to hide, he burst from cover in a diving roll, meeting the hunters with defensive fire. The six of them were running in a cluster when he started, Bolan rattling off a burst that tore one's throat to bloody tatters, while a second went down sprawling with a shoulder wound.

The others scattered, all firing as they ducked and ran, none of them taking time to aim. They might have tagged him, even so, but Bolan didn't offer them a stationary target. Rolling, firing, ever on the move, he caught a third man with a rising burst that gutted him and left him screaming on the ground.

That still left three in fighting form, and one who might recoup enough strength to rejoin the fight if Bolan gave him time. The soldier resolved that problem with a head shot for the gunner with the shoulder wound, pulling the plug on him as he was reaching for his gun.

The other three were running, ducking, firing hasty bursts at Bolan on the fly. One bullet tugged at his sleeve before he rolled out of the way, chasing the shooter with a 3-round burst that drilled him through the buttocks and left thigh.

Bolan's target scrabbled on the ground, bawling, and tried to turn his rifle toward the adversary who had wounded him. Given sufficient time, he might have made it, but his time was up. A second burst from Bolan hit the man's face, stretched him on the turf and left him shuddering into oblivion.

That left two shooters on their feet, circling to Bolan's right and left, while others still ran willy-nilly through the camp. Bolan needed to deal with those who hunted him, before their comrades caught on to the game in progress and decided to join in. If more came rushing to assist the two still on their feet, there was a good chance that he'd never find Naraka, much less make it home again.

The shooter looping to his right was closer, more aggressive, and the Executioner reacted first to him. Another roll to dodge incoming fire, then Bolan caught his enemy advancing. The man was startled when his rifle suddenly ran dry and he was forced to switch its magazine.

Too late.

The dazed expression on his target's face told Bolan that he recognized the end, even before the 5.56 mm manglers ripped into his chest and put him down. Swinging about to face the last contender, Bolan was surprised to find him fleeing, but he knew the guy would only carry word of an intruder in the camp, thus bringing reinforcements on the run.

Bolan lined up his shot and took it, squeezing off a burst that snapped his target's spine and sent him tumbling through a fairly decent somersault before he puddled on the grass, his life force spent. Bolan was up and moving in a flash, not giving anybody else the chance to pin him down, proceeding with his search.

And it paid off a heartbeat later, as he glimpsed Naraka just emerging from a tent, Mehadi resisting feebly as the poacher clutched her arm and jabbed her with the muzzle of his rifle.

They were headed for the forest, gaining speed, as Bolan started after them.

TAKERI WATCHED THE LAST man fall, no more than twenty feet in front of him, and marveled that none of the six had wounded him, despite their concentrated fire. It seemed to him a miracle of sorts, but at the moment he was hesitant to credit any deity with lending him a helping hand.

More likely demons, but he didn't want to think about that, either.

He was tired of hiding in the trees, sniping at targets from the shadows. It was safer, he supposed—one reason Cooper had assigned him to the secondary role, as well as keeping him out of the way—but he had no hope of locating Mehadi if he lingered in the forest out of reach and out of sight.

Before advancing into battle, he replaced his nearly empty magazine with a fresh one, made sure the rifle had a live round in its chamber, then prepared to move. None of the poachers still alive and on their feet were moving toward the spot where he was hidden, none apparently on guard against him. He would have a fair chance if he didn't dawdle, but ran straight into the fray.

Then do it! he urged himself.

Fear and something like exhilaration vied for primacy inside him, as Takeri left the trees and jogged into Naraka's camp past bodies scattered on the ground. On every side, the dead and wounded lay in twisted attitudes of suffering, some of them men he'd shot himself, and yet Takeri was not moved.

He was beyond that, a man removed from life as he had known it heretofore.

A poacher shouted at him in Hindi, "You there! Stop now!" Takeri spun to face him, found the man aiming a rifle at his face and fired before his enemy could squeeze the trigger. He saw bullets strike his adversary, blood spurting from chest and torso wounds before the gunman fell, his rifle tumbling from nerveless fingers.

How many was that? Takeri didn't know and hardly cared. If necessary, he could count the bodies later, but he had a hunch no one would ask. His time in the Sundarbans seemed almost outside of time, as if the bloody trek was being carried out in some bizarre parallel universe.

Takeri was surprised to see how few men still remained from Naraka's original crew. He hadn't killed that many, he was certain. Cooper had to have shot the rest, or maybe some had fled when they discovered that the fight had gone against them. Only five or six still moved about the camp, seeming disoriented, almost dazed.

No matter. They would have to die.

Takeri had the rifle at his shoulder, sighting on another target, when a woman's cry distracted him. He spun in time to see Naraka running toward the woods and dragging Mehadi after him, a weapon pressed into her side.

What should he do? he wondered.

Takeri didn't trust himself to make the shot, feared he would drop the woman while trying for Naraka at that distance, but he could not simply let them go. Instead of firing, then, he started after them, running, and something made him call out to the pair.

"Stop!" And then, as if saying her name would make a difference, "Indra!"

She faltered, missed a step and nearly fell, turning to glance over her shoulder at him. Hope or something like it blossomed on her face, before Naraka turned as well and saw Takeri. Snarling, tugging hard on Mehadi's arm, the poacher nearly dragged her off her feet, but she found her balance somehow and kept up with him.

Takeri feared he could not catch them, saw his only hope for rescue slipping through his fingers. Stopping short, he snapped the rifle to his shoulder once again and fought to frame Naraka in its sights. It was clear the poacher was a clever bastard, long accustomed to life on the run, dodging and ducking while he put the woman between them, used her body as a shield.

Takeri froze, his finger on the trigger and a bolt of fear blazed through him as a gunshot echoed through the camp. Downrange, he saw Naraka stumble, freeing Mehadi as he clutched his gun arm with the other hand. Takeri nearly dropped his rifle, certain that he hadn't fired, turning in the direction of the shot.

The big American was rushing forward, focused solely on the woman and the enemy in front of him.

Takeri sprinted toward the spot where Mehadi stood, rooted, apparently incapable of further flight. Naraka fired a burst toward Cooper, then another toward Takeri, snarling as he gave it up and bolted into the trees.

Takeri ducked and rolled, felt bullets whisper past him, then he reached Mehadi and pulled her down, begging to know if she was hurt.

"I'm fine," she answered dully, seeming almost in a trance.

"You're safe now," he assured her, turning to defend her from the poachers still upright and moving, while she answered from a distance, "Safe."

Beyond them, Cooper passed at speed, chasing Naraka toward the shadows puddled among the giant trees.

26

As the Executioner scrambled to his feet, he saw Takeri coming from his left, approaching Mehadi, scooping her into his arms. She seemed unharmed, but Bolan had no time to think about her at the moment. Racing past them on Naraka's track, he shouted at Takeri, "Watch the others!" He indicated with a vague wave of his left hand toward the three or four poachers still wandering around the stricken camp.

He hoped Mehadi would not distract Takeri to the point where both of them were killed by stragglers, but Naraka was his top priority. Somewhere ahead of Bolan, the outlaw was slipping through a forest that he knew as well as most people knew their own living rooms. It would be difficult—perhaps impossible—to find him, but the Executioner was not ready to quit.

For starters, he had blood to follow.

Not a lot of it, but one drop on a leaf told him that he was following Naraka's path. Another, on a stone some thirty feet ahead, assured him that he hadn't lost his quarry yet. Along the way, Bolan also discovered other traces of a man who'd put his faith in speed, rather than stealth. He spotted footprints and broken ferns, a scuff mark in the moss coating a mangrove's trunk, a stone gouged from its muddy bed by heavy boots.

Tracking was different from chasing. Both had as their goal the apprehension of specific prey, but one relied chiefly on speed, while the other involved reading clues—and often, as in this case, posed risks for the tracker if he was discovered by his prey.

In this case, the quarry was armed not with talons or fangs, but with an automatic weapon. Bolan's knowledge of the landscape was inferior to that of his intended prey, but he made up for that deficiency—or so he hoped—in jungle combat skill and training.

Furthermore, Naraka's wound, while relatively minor, aided Bolan in two ways. It helped to mark Naraka's trail, and it would slowly weaken him through loss of blood, while pain encumbered and distracted him. A seasoned fighting man could deal with that—bind up the wound to stop the blood flow, focus on the task at hand and soldier through the pain—but until Naraka brought himself around to that point, Bolan had an edge.

It wasn't much, but it was something.

And he needed all that he could get.

So focused was he on Naraka, that the Executioner required a conscious effort to recall the other dangers of the Sundarbans. Tigers and crocodiles. Cobras and quicksand. There were still at least a dozen ways for him to die, before he caught another glimpse of one of India's most-wanted fugitives. Each step he took was fraught with peril from above, below, on every side.

But Bolan's worst fear, at the moment, was that he might miss Naraka somehow, pass him by in hiding, while Naraka proved himself astute enough to trust his luck and hold his fire. At what point should he call the search a bust and waste of time? Sundown? Midnight? A week from Tuesday?

Realistically, Bolan knew that if he hadn't found Naraka by the time night fell over the Sundarbans, he would've lost his chance. Even that distant deadline begged the question: how far should he wander from Naraka's camp when he ran out of clues and markers on the trail? If he deserted Mehadi and Takeri without bringing down his quarry, what would he have accomplished?

He noticed another spot of blood, so small he'd almost missed it while a portion of his mind was elsewhere. Bolan focused on the narrow, almost ghostly trail with everything he had, concentrating fully. Any measure of distraction could prove fatal, and Bolan had no mental energy to spare for questions while he stalked a killer through the forest.

He was stooping to inspect a scuff mark in the mud, perhaps a heel print, when a rifle shot rang out and sent him lunging facedown in the weeds.

NARAKA MOUTHED A SILENT curse and fired a second shot. His wounded, trembling arm had spoiled the first. He knew the difference between a dive and a fall, knew that the first shot had not touched his target.

Nor the second, seemingly, as automatic fire ripped through the undergrowth, too close for comfort, forcing him to spin and lunge away. Naraka stumbled in the process, fell hard on his wounded arm, and bit his tongue to keep from blurting out a curse that might betray him.

This man was no easy mark. With only one or two others, it seemed that he'd wiped out Naraka's team of hunters and their camp, thereby undoing years of work. Now he was bent on finishing the job with one more kill.

No matter, Naraka told himself. When he'd disposed of this one, he could build a new organization, better and stronger than the one he'd lost. New contacts in Calcutta would be needed, but that never seemed to be a problem when large sums of money were concerned.

This time next month, Naraka estimated, he'd be back in business, doing better than before the stranger dropped into his life. Meanwhile, he would survive by living off the land and from the generosity of villagers who loved or feared him.

But he had to kill the deadly stranger first.

Naraka crawled through ferns and tall grass like a lizard, trying not to make unnecessary noise. After each move, he paused to listen, straining ears that rang from gunfire in the camp to catch a hint of where his enemy had gone, what he was doing, whether he was lying wounded in the forest or approaching, inch by inch.

Nothing.

Naraka knew that he would have to draw his adversary out, present himself as bait to bring the warrior within striking range. A glimpse was all he needed, but—

The sound of footsteps, when it came, surprised Naraka. It was coming from the wrong direction, farther back, in the direction of the camp he'd lately fled. Naraka knew his enemy wasn't that far away, nor would he draw fire with such plodding progress through the forest.

But if not the white man…who?

Naraka waited, every sense on full alert. He strained his ears, refused to blink, even tried sniffing the faint breeze that wafted toward him from the general direction of his camp. It carried the familiar smells of cordite, smoke, and the metallic scent of fresh-spilled blood. As for distinguishing an individual, it did no good at all.

Naraka found himself clutching his rifle so tightly that his knuckles ached. Slowly, reluctantly, he let his grip relax. The man approaching him—and there was only one, his ears still told him that much—might be friend or foe. A straggler from the camp, or a companion of the white man who was bent on killing him.

In either case, the harsh sound of his footsteps told Naraka that he'd given little thought to living out the afternoon.

Naraka turned, only a fraction of an inch, to face the steadily advancing sounds. It seemed to take forever, raising his weapon to brace the stock against his shoulder, painfully aware that any sudden move might make him visible to his committed enemy.

John Smith, the girl had called him. An American.

The other one, glimpsed briefly as Naraka fled the camp, would be Kalari. He was a native, likely from Calcutta. When Naraka had secured his new position and resumed his hunting, there'd be time enough to deal with that one.

Unless he was moving toward the slaughter immediately.

Naraka spotted the new arrival, recognized his face and put a name to it. He was Panu Nadisu, a young man who'd joined Naraka's band a year earlier. He was a veteran of many hunts and several sniping raids against the government, but he'd seen nothing like the bloodshed of this afternoon.

Naraka saw that Nadisu was shaken. He wasn't following Naraka's trail, it seemed, but simply fleeing the battle zone. Unknowingly, he was about to make a target of himself for the American.

Naraka could have warned Nadisu, but decided it did not serve his purpose. When his adversary shot Nadisu, he would give himself away. Naraka would strike then, and finish it. Move on from there to find the new life of adventure that was waiting for him as an outlaw in the Sundarbans.

Poised to fire at anything that moved, he watched Nadisu drawing closer, step by careless plodding step. The American would take him soon, or let him get away.

Was that the plan? Was Smith so disciplined that he would let an easy target pass him by, while waiting for Naraka to expose himself?

A clever bastard, this one, He thought. But—

The rush came unexpectedly, stunning Naraka with its ferocity. But it was not a man in camouflage fatigues who pounded upon Panu Nadisu, crushing him to the earth before he could defend himself.

It was a tiger, roaring at the final moment of the kill to freeze its startled prey, while gaping jaws with three-inch fangs snapped shut around Nadisu's head.

THE EXECUTIONER had tracked the straggler from Naraka's camp, hoping but not expecting that Naraka would break cover, call to the approaching man for help. He'd waited as the young man came within forty feet, then planned to let him pass untouched rather than announcing his position while he stalked Naraka through the forest.

But it didn't work that way.

The tiger came from nowhere, springing from a murky wall of vines and shadows. The great cat sprang upon the newcomer as he passed by its hiding place, claws and fangs embedded in his flesh before the gunman had a chance to scream.

Whatever sounds he made beyond that point were literally swallowed by the tiger. Wide jaws clamped around the man's face while it shook him like a rag doll, snarling all the while.

Bolan assumed the man was dead—hoped so, for his sake—as the tiger tugged and twisted his head. He hadn't heard the poacher's neck snap, but the angle of his head showed it had to be broken. Even if he clung to life he would be numb and thus spared the agony of claws raking his chest to bloody ribbons.

Bolan could have shot the cat from where he crouched, behind a looming mangrove tree, but that would have meant showing where he was to save a dead man. He knew Naraka wouldn't hesitate to take advantage of the lapse, while leaving his subordinate to the tiger.

Bolan watched and waited while the cat, convinced at last that it had scored a kill, began to drag its lifeless prey into the woods. It would be gone within another moment, maybe haul its kill a hundred yards or more before it settled down to feed, and then—

In retrospect, he never knew exactly why Naraka chose that moment to emerge from hiding. Maybe the young man killed by the tiger was a friend. Maybe the poacher wanted the big cat. Perhaps something had snapped inside him and he couldn't have explained the move himself.

In any case, Naraka broke from cover with a shout, a roar, almost the equal of the tiger's. Brandishing a rifle, he chose not to fire it at the cat, but triggered two quick shots into the humid air, instead, then rushed the tiger from behind.

Whether the cat knew other human beings had been watching the whole time or not, it turned upon Naraka as if startled by his presence. Maybe it was his audacity that shocked the cat into releasing its limp prey and turning on the man who had destroyed so many of its kind.

The tiger studied Naraka for perhaps two seconds, during which the poacher kept advancing, with his rifle held across his chest. He didn't fire or even aim, instead berating his four-footed enemy in scathing language Bolan couldn't understand. Curses, perhaps, or one last challenge for supremacy.

The tiger cocked its head, then roared and launched itself into a headlong charge. Naraka seemed to second-guess himself in that split second, but it was too late to turn and run. Instead, he stood his ground and snapped the rifle to his shoulder, leaning into target acquisition as the tiger barreled toward him, striped flanks pumping with exertion, jaws agape and tail held high.

Naraka almost made it.

The tiger leaped into the air just as Naraka fired. From Bolan's viewpoint, it appeared to turn in midair, twisting underneath the weapon's muzzle as the flash of gunfire scorched its flank. Its forepaws struck Naraka in the chest, the tiger's massive weight forcing him to the ground.

Naraka fought the tiger like the jungle denizen he was. His rifle sailed beyond his reach after the first shot, but he groped to reach a dagger sheathed on his left hip, while fending off the cat's jaws with his right hand, fingers lost inside the gnashing maw.

The poacher's first scream was a shrill, almost unearthly sound. Perhaps it was the sight of the great cat devouring his hand and starting on his forearm, or the knowledge that his life would be snuffed out by one of the same creatures he'd mercilessly hunted for the past decade or more. In any case, he kicked and bellowed at the tiger, bucking underneath it, while claws ripped his flesh, and blood sprayed from his wounds across the mossy turf.

Bolan had a clear shot. It was clear in the sense that he could riddle both combatants if he chose, without a thought to rescuing Naraka from the cat.

Rising from his crouch, he let the Steyr's muzzle drop until it pointed at the ground between his feet. He kept his finger on the trigger, just in case, but made no move to interrupt the struggle being acted out before him.

As Naraka reached his knife, baring its blade, the tiger spit out the arm and turned to meet the thrust. Its head ducked, yawning jaws closed on Naraka's left forearm. The poacher lacked the strength to scream as the hunting knife slipped from his twitching fingers and was lost.

The tiger turned and bent to grasp Naraka's face between its jaws. A final scream was muffled by the jaws and throat, as if a pillow had been pressed over Naraka's face.

Bolan turned from the sight but couldn't block the sound as long, sharp fangs punched through Naraka's cheekbones and his face imploded, crushed between the tiger's jaws. A final, frenzied thrashing sound marked the conclusion of the battle, with Naraka's heels thumping the turf in clumsy little dance steps.

When the tremors ceased, the tiger shook him once more, then released him for a moment. Glancing back across its shoulder toward the first man it had killed, the cat considered which would make the better meal. At last, it chose Naraka, gripped him by the throat and dragged him out of sight into the forest.

Bolan gave the great cat ample time to clear the area, and held his rifle ready as he started back toward camp.

Epilogue

Calcutta

"It is sad that you must leave us," Indra Mehadi said. Takeri, sitting close beside her in the international airport's departure lounge, frowned slightly but made no comment.

"It's time," Bolan replied. "I started wearing out my welcome here the minute I arrived."

"For safety's sake, Indra," Takeri said. "He knows what's best."

"But the authorities—"

"Are better off not knowing I was ever here," Bolan reminded her. "You're both safe now. Naraka's out of business. They can work on something else."

"It's bad to say, I know," Mehadi said, "but we must be grateful that Naraka killed Americans and brought you here. Without you, I would certainly be dead, and Naraka would be killing as before."

"The main thing is that you have justice for your parents," Bolan said. "That is, if you let it go."

She nodded, hesitant at first, then with a greater certainty after she met Takeri's gaze and gripped his hand. "I think so, yes. It was a burden that I took upon myself, when others might have done a better job. I won't make that mistake again."

With any luck, Bolan thought, you won't have to.

"That's best for all concerned, I think," he said.

Takeri checked his watch against a nearby television screen and saw that Bolan's flight would not begin to board for twenty minutes. Reaching for a comment that would keep their conversation from stagnating, he asked Bolan, "Have you followed any of the news reports since we got back?"

"No," Bolan replied.

"Authorities in West Bengal have called for new offensives against banditry and poaching in the Sundarbans. We've heard all this before, of course, but maybe this time the publicity will help sustain momentum for a time."

"I know our game wardens would love to have you stay here," Mehadi blurted out, then flushed, embarrassed.

"They might," Bolan said, "but their superiors wouldn't be thrilled about it, I can promise you."

Takeri held her hand in both of his. "Indra—"

"I only meant...well...never mind."

"We found ourselves in a peculiar situation," Bolan said. "It wasn't business as usual, and it barely worked this time. You had a close call, as it was."

"What is this 'close call'?" she asked. Takeri said something in Hindi and she nodded, saying, "Yes. It was called closely. Mr. Cooper, if you had not been there—"

"Then you likely wouldn't have been in that mess to start with. And I nearly missed you at the end," he said, rewriting history to suit the moment. "It was Abhaya who found you, don't forget."

Mehadi clutched Takeri's hand more tightly, beaming a smile that had to have warmed his heart and other organs. "No," she said. "I'm not forgetting anything."

Some things were better off forgotten, Bolan thought, but kept it to himself. They hadn't talked about Mehadi's interrogation—well, *he* hadn't talked to her about it—but she didn't seem to be bogged down in any kind of posttraumatic stress.

To Bolan's eyes, Mehadi seemed stronger than she had the night they met, no small tribute to her resilience and determination.

"In fact," she added, almost as an afterthought, "I think that being placed in danger may have been a blessing in disguise."

Takeri squirmed a little in his seat, but Bolan saw that he was proud and dying for a chance to let it out. "Indra," he said, "I hope you may…that is, I pray you will…um…"

"All in time," she told him. "Never fear."

Acutely conscious of the three's-a-crowd rule, Bolan counted off a long moment of silence, then inquired, "So, Abhaya, will you still be working with the Company?"

It was the closest he could come to any cloak-and-dagger reference, not knowing what Takeri had told Mehadi of his life during their private moments.

"I think it's best if I find other work," Takeri said. "Something more stable. Less provocative. This was my last adventure, I believe."

"Well, maybe this kind, anyway," Bolan replied. It earned him one of Mehadi's smiles. "What were you thinking of, as a replacement?"

"Something in security, perhaps," Takeri said, "or the administrative side of law enforcement."

"He could even study law and run for office," Mehadi said.

"No thank you," Takeri said. "I have seen enough political corruption for a lifetime."

"But you'd change all that," Mehadi replied, speaking with the simple faith of one in love or well along the road toward getting there.

"I'm not so sure," Takeri said. "*It* might change *me*."

"I wouldn't let that happen," she told him.

The expression on Takeri's face told Bolan the young woman had said everything Takeri longed to hear in those five words.

"Well, if I'm ever back this way, you'll get my vote," Bolan remarked.

Takeri puzzled over that and said, "Unless you are a citizen, you cannot—"

Mehadi pinched his arm, saying, "It is a joke Abhaya."

"Ah. Of course, I knew that."

Now it was Bolan's turn to check his watch, hoping his flight would start to board before he caught a case of sugar shock. He wished the couple well, sincerely, but their new relationship comprised a part of life that Bolan had foresworn when he turned from the U.S. Army to a lonely path of War Everlasting.

His homeland's conflicts ran their course, began and ended, but the war Bolan had chosen for himself went on interminably, with new adversaries popping up each time he scored a victory. The faces and the motives changed, but there were always predators enough to go around.

Always a new crusade to occupy the Executioner.

It did him good to see young lovers now and then. They helped remind Bolan what he was fighting for—a world where innocence survived, albeit under siege, and where such goodness had a fighting chance. Unfortunately, since most innocents weren't world-class warriors in their own right, they required assistance from a seasoned fighting man.

And Bolan fit the bill, in spades.

At last his flight was called and Bolan rose, lifting a carry-on that held no weapons. He felt naked when unarmed, after the years of constant warfare, but security was tight and he supposed no one would try to kill him on the plane.

Takeri shook his hand and Mehadi hugged him, holding on a moment longer than Takeri would've liked, then he was out of there and moving rapidly along the jet way to his aircraft, without looking back.

Forget me, Bolan thought, *and live your lives.*

It would be better, all around.